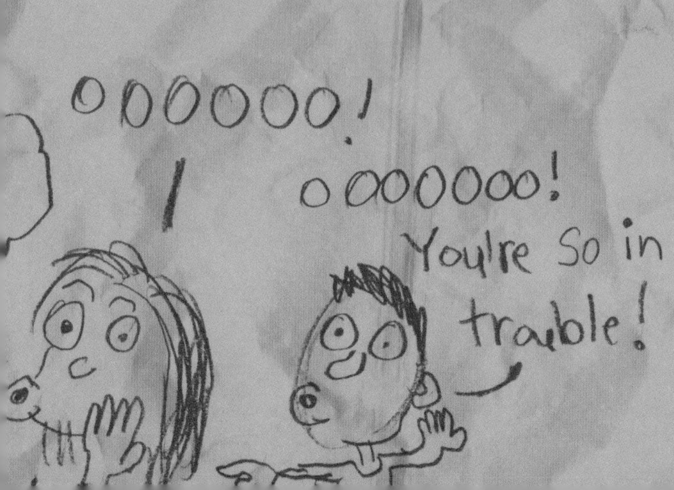
OOOOOO!
OOOOOOO!
You're So in trauble!

DESMOND PUCKET

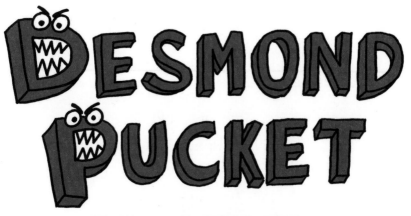

MAKES MONSTER MAGIC

Other books by Mark Tatulli

DESMOND PUCKET

MAKES MONSTER MAGIC

**Andrews McMeel
Publishing, LLC**

Kansas City • Sydney • London

1 THERE GOES DESMOND

"Mom! Mo-o-o-o-o-o-mmmm . . ."

I groan in my best I'm-about-to-blow-chow voice.

Mom knows the sound well from all the late-night fevers throughout the years, when she held my puking head.

I hear a stirring down the hall. Then my mom's familiar clunky footsteps on autopilot as she makes her way to my room, flipping on light switches as she goes.

Mom pushes through my door and comes to my bedside, her face full of concern.

"What is it, Des? Are you sick?"

I make gurgly noises.

I spit blood.

A large red stain spreads across my belly as a claw rips through my shirt and a slimy, multi-eyed, many-fanged creature breaks out of my stomach with a screech, its tentacles jiggling and blood spurting from the gaping hole!

She's so on to me.

"We'll talk about this more in the morning, mister," Mom says as she stomps out of the room, huffing that mom-huff that all mothers learn at mom training school.

Mom can say a lot with one huff. That one was the famous you're-on-my-last-nerve huff. And it's probably not a good idea to make my mother huffing mad right now.

Because Mom's the one person keeping me from getting kicked out of Cloverfield Memorial Junior High School!

2 FOR THE LOVE OF MONSTERS

I guess I should explain.

My name is Desmond Pucket, and as you probably already guessed, I'm into all kinds of scary stuff. I'm a Professor of Frightology, with a Master's in Monsters. Or, as I like to call myself . . .

"Gourmet of Gore"

← My official Logo

Someday I'm going to be rich and famous for creating the most amazing and horrifying amusement park haunted house rides ever! That's my dream!

Maybe I'll even make something greater than the biggest haunted dark ride in the whole world, the **MOUNTAIN FULL OF MONSTERS** at Crab Shell Pier!

I design, draw, and create all of my own scary-monster effects . . .

The most awesome
dark ride ever

Brochure I saved from
when I was little

Like my math teacher, Mrs. Raup, says, "If you could draw your lessons, Desmond, you'd be a straight-A student!" Those were her exact words when she handed me back my last test, with the Stomach Screecher drawn on the back of page two . . . and a big fat F at the top of page one.

I'm not rich and famous yet, either. I'm only in junior high, and my weird hobby makes grown-ups nervous. Especially teachers and important-looking bald guys with half glasses and vomit green sweaters, also known as school officials.

I'm not sure what it is that makes them "official" . . . Maybe it's those vomit green sweaters. Maybe those special sweaters are handed out in some secret ceremony.

It's not that I'm a bad kid. I've never hurt anyone. And I've never gotten into any real trouble . . . not until this year, anyway. But suddenly my special "monstery interest" is getting more attention and I'm skating on thin ice.

Now Mom is the only thing standing between me and getting tossed by the vomit-green-sweater wearers!

OK, to tell this right, I think I have to go back in time a bit. See, this all really started a few years ago . . .

3 THE DARK RIDE OF CRAB SHELL PIER

I was only seven years old at the time, but I knew that Crab Shell Amusement Pier was going to suck eggs big-time.

Our whole family really wanted to go to Wizz Dizzy World in Florida. But back then, Dad was still finishing up school and we didn't have tons of money for big, expensive vacations. So we settled for a road trip to Crab Shell Pier.

That actually should be their TV commercial:

It didn't matter to my older sister, Rachel, that we were going to a cruddy substitute for Wizz Dizzy World. She already had a boyfriend, and her little pea brain was completely crammed full with dreams of Dennis. We could have been going cow tipping at DairyLand for all she cared.

But I was miffed.

Wizz Dizzy World in Florida had just opened a new 3-D Virtual Alien Attack attraction ("attraction" is theme park-ese for "really expensive ride").

And I was missing it.

Dad was too busy keeping track of turnpike exits to sense my mood. But Mom knew and tried to get me excited.

I did one of those eye-rolly smiles to let Mom know she was getting into kid territory she knew nothing about, but Mom's no dummy. She already knew that fast rides are OK but nothing tops a 3-D Virtual Alien Attack attraction. I had to give Mom points for trying, though.

When we got to Crab Shell Pier, the place was an explosion of noise, flashing lights, and giant swooshing rides; it smelled like old hot dogs, burnt french fries, gasoline engines, and wet boardwalk wood.

Definitely not Wizz Dizzy World.

But then I saw it, way down at the very end of the pier . . .

. . . the most awesomely fantastic and freaky triple-decker dark ride in the whole entire world.

I looked at Mom, but she was already off buying tickets. We inched our way forward in line, and I heard the screams of the kids inside the giant fake mountain as their pretzel cars rattled over the three stories of tracks, running in and out of the glorious monster-packed caves. I felt that thrilled/scared/excited tingle as we got closer.

Finally, it was our turn. The rickety little car pulled up in front of us.

Dark ride Cars are called Pretzel cars because of the way they move.

They turn and twist like a Pretzel!

And that's when I saw *the CREATURE* . . .

Man, I hate those smiley characters, holding one cartoon gloved hand over my head, laughing at me! Every one of those goofy signs was a reminder I was small for my age. I was totally crushed! I stepped out of line as all the bigger kids pushed by and snickered.

Dad and Rachel still went on the ride, but Mom stayed with me. She held her arm around me and said nothing.

This, of course, was all incredibly funny to Rachel, who towered over me . . .

So I had a hard time feeling sorry for her when a kid on the Tilt-a-Whirl actually did barf in her lap.

Even though I didn't get on the big ride, the day wasn't a total waste.

But I knew one day I would return to Crab Shell Pier! And I would go on that Mountain Full of Monsters ride! I swore it!

And now that day is almost here—the sixth-grade class trip—and I can't believe I'm in trouble of missing out again!

All because of my little pranks . . .

4 DESMOND'S GREATEST HITS

Everybody has at least one great school moment, right? Like the time you climb to the top of the rope in gym and ring the bell and everybody is watching, especially Tina Schimsky.

Or when you rescue the girls from jail (including Tina Schimsky) during a game of Capture the Flag and actually capture the flag.

Or the day you're the hero of dodgeball, jumping in front of Tina Schimsky, catching the ball that Scott Seltzer aimed at her, and winning the game.

Well, none of that happened to me.

One of my greatest moments was the shrieking rubber goblin in the teachers' lounge toilet.

A Desmond Pucket design # 92
The Toilet Goblin
Goblin attached to seat
When toilet is opened, Goblin Come's Out!

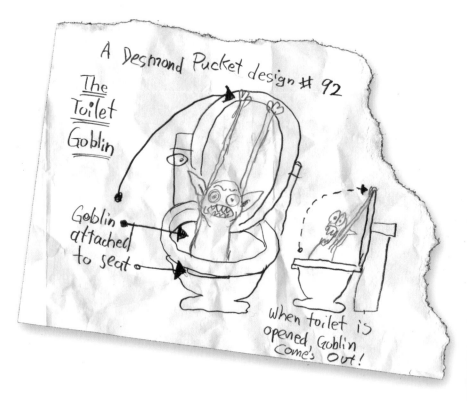

I didn't actually see the whole thing go down, but Jon Cahill was in the teachers' lounge dropping a book off to Mr. Landrum, and he said it was pretty obvious why Mrs. Rubin was the chorus teacher.

And then Mr. Landrum screamed when he saw Mrs. Rubin without her wig.

Score!

And who could forget the bloody cakes in Home Ec? Ricky DiMarco had to help me with that one. Every top effects man has a number-two guy he can totally trust to get the job done, and Ricky is as good as it gets.

OK, so Ricky is no rocket scientist, either. He's not even qualified to be a paper airplane scientist. He's more of a jokes-and-gags man of the whoopee cushion/plastic vomit variety.

Ricky and I met back in the fourth grade. One day we just started tossing balled-up scrap paper cartoons back and forth in class, trying to make each other laugh and get in trouble with the teacher.

This is one of the first cartoons Ricky ever tossed to me:

It cracked me up so much that Mr. McGeorge gave me a week of detention. Me and Ricky have been best friends ever since.

When we're old enough to drive, me and Ricky are getting jobs at Crab Shell Pier. Of course I want to work on the Mountain Full of Monsters ride, but Ricky wants to be in the dunker tank. You know, that guy who insults people who then try to knock him into the water?

I know a lot of teachers who will be lining up for that.

So anyway, back to the bloody cakes in Home Ec . . . definitely one of my ideas that was right up Ricky's alley.

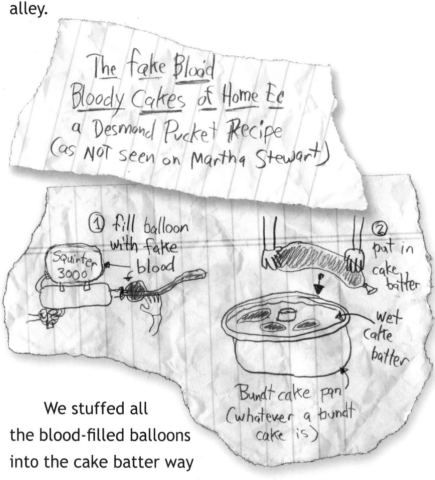

The fake Blood
Bloody Cakes of Home Ec
a Desmond Pucket Recipe
(as NOT seen on Martha Stewart)

① fill balloon with fake blood

Squirter 3000

② put in cake batter

wet cake batter

Bundt cake pan (whatever a bundt cake is)

We stuffed all the blood-filled balloons into the cake batter way before the Home Ec kids and the teacher got back from lunch to bake it. We didn't know what the cakes were for, which made for a very special coffee break during Back-to-School Night . . .

I don't think any of those parents and teachers will ever eat cake again!

And then there were the giant worms in the cafetorium . . . definitely a gold star moment!

Someday I'll tell you how hard it was to keep battery-operated rubber worms wriggling in hot mashed potatoes.

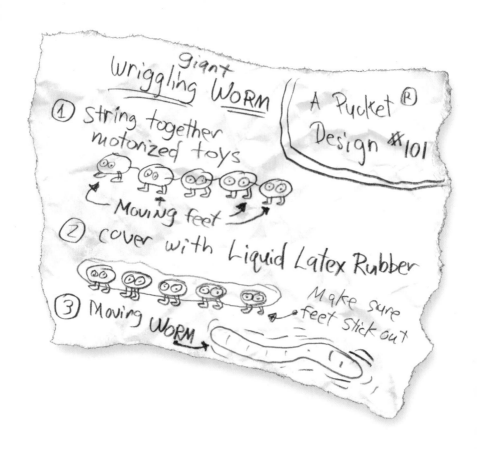

But getting one over on that sourpants lunch lady Mrs. Belkman was worth the whole secret setup and almost getting caught.

The greatest part was when she freaked and dropped the entire sheet of mashed potatoes on the floor right in front of Scott Seltzer . . .

... who screamed like a little baby-man. Classic!

The really terrible part of all these triumphs is I can't take any credit for them.

If I did, I'd get kicked out of school right away. Cloverfield Memorial Junior High has a "zero-tolerance" policy . . . which means that the teachers have zero tolerance for goblins in their toilets and worms in their taters.

Of course, they all sort of knew I was the man behind the magic. They just couldn't prove it.

And nobody wants to prove it more than Mr. Needles.

Mr. Needles

Coca-cola Brown Aviator glasses

Kinky, wavy dyed hair - looks like old Harry Houdini pictures

doggie jowls

Rolled-up sleeves means business

Actually makes growling noises

mud brown pants (matches glasses)

High waters

5 MR. NEEDLES

Mr. Needles is the head of the disciplinary office at Cloverfield Junior High and the king of all school officials. He's the one I always visit after all my triumphs.

And I usually get the standard warning talk from him, with something like "You better buckle down, son" or "Time to straighten out and fly right, mister . . ."

I'm pretty sure somewhere in his office Mr. Needles has a book like this:

THE OFFICIAL
SCHOOL OFFICIAL'S
COMPLETE Book
OF
LAME-O
EXPRESSIONS

I always try to stay one step ahead of Mr. Needles. I'm careful never to leave any evidence, and it's pretty easy to hear him coming in his clompy brown dress shoes. So Mr. Needles can't ever prove anything.

All he has are the warnings and threats, which he always ends with:

Well, he's right. I almost got caught that last time with the giant wriggly worms in the mashed potatoes. So I have to lie low. I'll put my exploding zombie head project on hold. For now, I'll control my inner monster.

But, dang, it's really hard for me to squash my scaring instincts!

It's not natural!

Especially when there's someone who's really asking for it . . .

. . . like **RACHEL!**

6 THE FABULOUS RACHEL

You might think it's great to have a popular older sister, that you're all set, right? She's queen of the school, so maybe some of that popularity might trickle down to you. And then you'll be accepted by the "in" crowd right away because your sister is already there, and older sisters always look out for younger brothers. Right? Right??

Unless your sister is Rachel.

Rachel wants it all, and she expects everyone else to make it their life's work to bring her the rest of the all that she doesn't have. She gets everything she wants. It makes sense, I suppose, because Rachel's a lot more work than I am. Mom always says, "The squeaky wheel gets the oil," and my sister never stops squeaking.

I guess it's kind of my own fault Rachel hates me. When we were younger, I practiced my "plastic surgery" on her dolls. Pretty Pony and Ken were the first to go under the knife.

And the Little Mermaid soon became . . .

Rachel's record-breaking collection of Barbie dolls made an awesome mob of zombies.

(The most stylish zombies ever, I have to say.)

And there's something cute about Molly the American Girl doll covered in werewolf hair:

Let's not even talk about the Polly Pocket Chamber of Horrors.

But Rachel never appreciated my creativity, then or now. And so there's always lots and lots of Rachel squeaking.

Whenever Rachel sees me, she grimaces her bracified teeth and rolls her over-mascarafied eyes. And since our grades are worlds apart, we pretty much ignore each other.

But now something's happening that I can't ignore:

OMG!

You are SO invited to Rachel's Slumber Party!

gift

I know—is that the ugliest party invitation ever, or what? Did she use every piece of cruddy clip art from the whole entire Internet?

A slumber party!

With tons of screechy girls!

And presents!

Well, that's Rachel.

Which is another reason I don't feel bad risking it all to do what I gotta do . . .

7 THE SCARE-FEST EXTRAVAGANZA

Picture it: Rachel and thirteen other squealing, bracified, and over-mascarafied girls in one place. At night. Lights off. Telling scary slasher stories.

IT IS MY DUTY TO MAKE SOME MONSTER MAGIC!

I know what I have to do. I can't resist.

It will be my masterpiece!

OK, now, I know I said I have to lie low and keep my nose clean because Mr. Needles is watching me . . . but this isn't school! This is a sleepover party packed with stupid, ready-to-scare eighth-grade girls! What kind of monster maker would let that opportunity slip by?

So I carefully draw up my plans . . .

. . . plotting out every creepy sound effect and bugaboo . . .

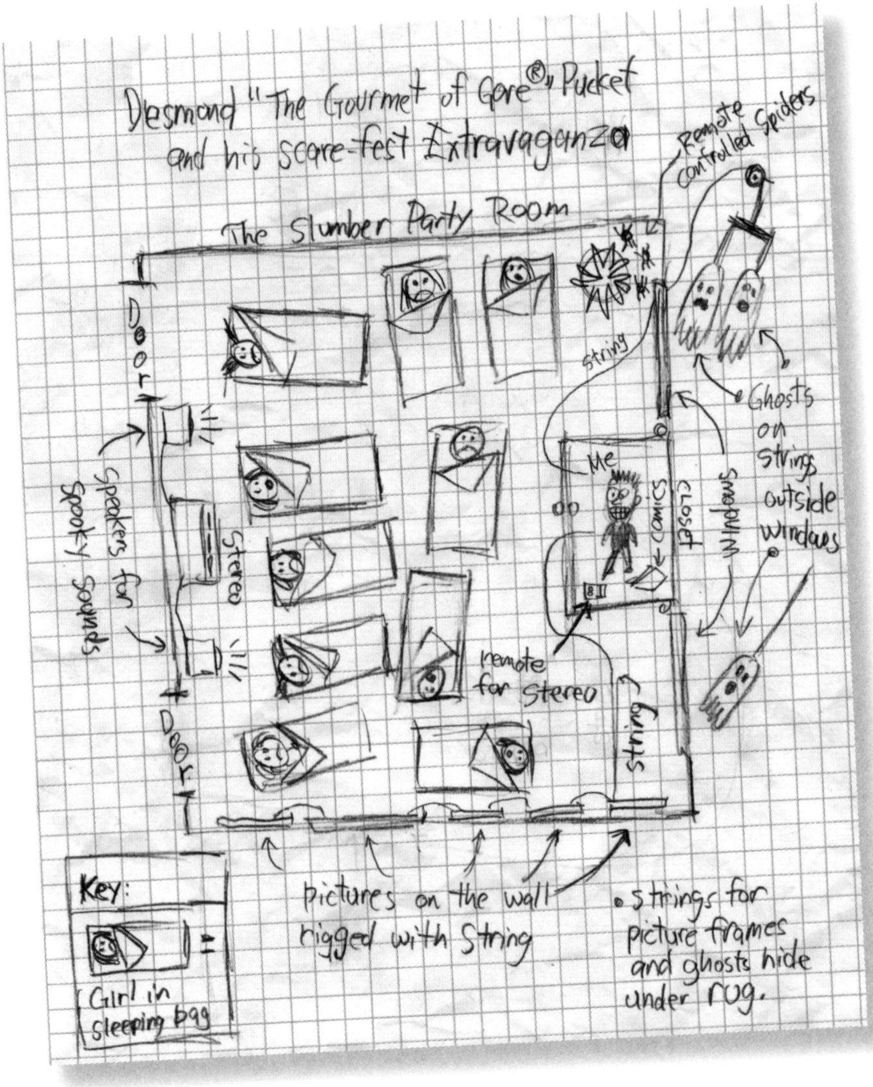
Desmond "The Gourmet of Gore®" Pucket
and his scare-fest Extravaganza
The Slumber Party Room
Remote controlled Spiders
Door
Door
String
Ghosts on strings outside windows
Windows
Closet
Comics
Me
Speakers for Spooky Sounds
Stereo
remote for Stereo
String
Pictures on the wall rigged with String
Strings for picture frames and ghosts hide under rug.
Key:
= Girl in sleeping bag

Then, way before the party starts, I hide in a closet in the slumber party room and wait.

And I wait.

And wait.

And fart.

I suddenly realize what a small closet this is.

Finally, I hear the girls' giggly, goofy voices as they pile into the room. I peek out and see them in their multicolored animal-print pajamas, all carrying their favorite stuffed monkey or HiDeeHo-Hippo doll or giant banana pillow. And then they chatter away for hours about boys . . . who's a dork, who's a babe, and who's a blah, blah, blahddy, blee, blah . . .

After a long while, the girls finally settle down. Someone turns the lights off. Things are starting to happen! I can feel my excitement building.

I hear the quiet voice of Nadine Templeton as she begins the most perfectly awesome and scary ghost story ever, the one story that legally *must* be told at every slumber party . . .

Now, there's a bunch of different ways that the Bloody Mary story can go:

Or:

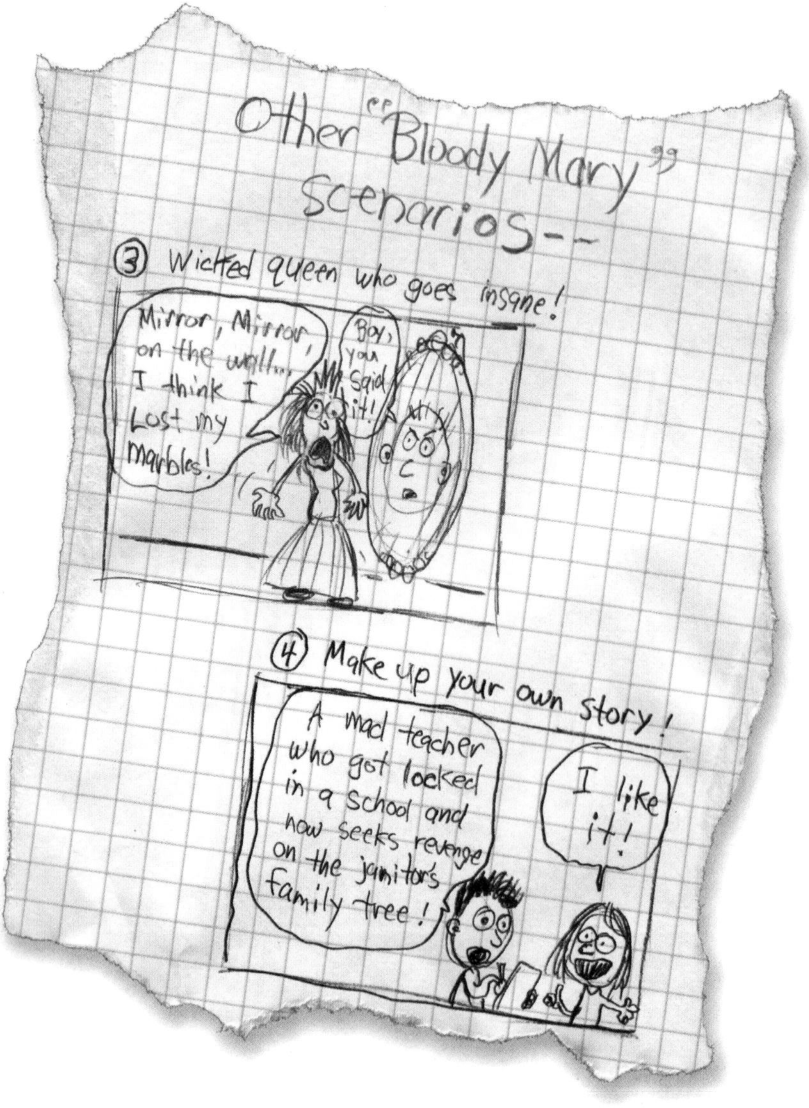

Other "Bloody Mary" Scenarios--
③ Wicked queen who goes insane!
Mirror, Mirror, on the wall... I think I Lost my marbles!
Boy, you said it!
④ Make up your own story!
A mad teacher who got locked in a School and now seeks revenge on the janitor's family tree!
I like it!

Well, you get the idea.

As long as death, blood, and a lady out for revenge are involved, the Bloody Mary story works. Now, after the story is told, you're supposed to stand in front of a mirror and turn around thirteen times, all the while chanting the name . . .

. . . and when you stop, you open your eyes and look in the mirror, and Bloody Mary will appear! And then . . .

Well, nobody really knows exactly what happens then, because the way the thing usually goes is the way it's going right now: all the girls start to do it and then chicken out before finishing the mirror bit. The giggles and tiny screams are becoming more nervous. And the fear-o-meter is beeping off the charts!

The timing is perfect . . .

At first the girls fall silent. Then they start making small scared noises. I release the net full of rubber creepy-crawlers and motorized spiders. And the ghosts on the strings. And start rocking picture frames.

Finally, I burst out of the closet!

The girls freeze.

They stare at me.

Eyes the size of ping-pong balls.

And after a second of open-mouthed shock, all hoo-ha breaks loose!

The girls run in all different directions, crashing into one another, knocking over cups of BubbleBurp soda, stepping into popcorn bowls, and slipping on greasy corn chip bags, the whole time screaming one ginormous scream. Then the front door bangs open and they all run out.

And I activate phase two of the plan.

Yes, we save the best for last . . . the icing on the cake!

And the girls take off at top speed, waving their arms and screaming down our once quiet street.

All except for Rachel . . .

. . . who stays behind to pummel me with a HiDeeHo-Hippo.

But at least Ricky makes a clean getaway.

All the gimmicks and haunted effects worked perfectly, especially my newest creation . . .

All in all, an awesomely successful night!

Unfortunately, my dad and I have very different ideas about the definition of *"successful."*

8 ONE DISAPPOINTED DAD

DESMOND, I'M VERY **DISAPPOINTED**.

Dad is a master with that D-word. He only pulls it out when he absolutely needs it. Kind of like a pinch hitter. Or a really giant chain saw. And it hurts much worse.

My father is a serious man. And like all serious men, he became a dentist. A well-respected dentist.

That cracks me up. I mean, "well-respected" and "person who puts his hands in other peoples' mouths"? Always makes me laugh.

And they say I'm weird?!

Don't get me wrong. I love the guy, and having a dentist dad isn't all bad. For someone in my line of work, a dentist's office is a treasure chest of plastic tubes, latex gloves, rubber bulbs, and all sorts of dental sculpting stuff great for molding made-to-order fangs. It's a monster-effects man's dream!

And you want to talk about jagged, monstery teeth?! My dad has plaster casts of his patients' teeth that make the goblins in *The Lord of the Rings* look like supermodels!

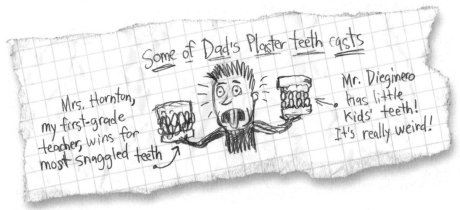

Some of Dad's Plaster teeth casts

Mrs. Hornton, my first-grade teacher, wins for most snaggled teeth →

Mr. Dieginero has little kids' teeth! It's really weird!

Anyway, in our gabby little town, a well-respected dentist (I just giggled again) doesn't need a weirdo monster-loving son messing things up for him. So Dad is the first to suggest something serious has to be done about "The Desmond Situation," as he lovingly refers to me.

And my luck is only getting better. One of the girls running from Rachel's pajama party fell and chipped a tooth. In a small town like ours, that makes me almost an accomplice to murder.

Plus, another girl had an asthma attack, so it's like a double homicide. Oh, and did I mention that other girl just happened to be . . . Leesa Needles?

That's right, Mr. Needles's daughter!

9 MOM TO THE RESCUE

Before Dad can figure out the perfect punishment, Mr. Needles jumps into action. Mr. Needles finally has the proof he needs. And he's so serious this time, he has "The Desmond Situation" brought before the school board! Yes! The board!

OK, I'm not exactly sure what "the board" is, but it's pretty dang serious when the board has something brought before it. The board gets cranky when things are in front of it. And this particular board has had enough of me.

Now it's up to Mom to save the day!

Mom is the only person who understands what my weird hobby means to me. So she battles it out with the cranky school board and Mr. Needles and all the sweatery officials, and even the town's most well-respected dentist . . .

. . . and comes up with a Mom solution to "The Desmond Situation" that makes everyone happy.

Everyone except Mr. Needles.

See, Mr. Needles really just wants to boot me out of school for good. His goal is to ship me off to Wood Hook Junior High on the other side of town. That's where they send all the Cloverfield rejects.

And since he didn't get his way this time, he makes me a vow . . .

OK, he didn't say that exactly, but it was something witchy like that. And I know from now on, Mr. Needles will be watching me closer than ever before.

But who cares about Mr. Needles? Thanks to Mom, I get to stay at Cloverfield! And that means I get to go on the sixth-grade field trip to Crab Shell Pier! Woo-hoo!

Still, I know some kind of punishment is coming. And even though Mom and the school board and all the school officials agree on what to do about me, Dad volunteers to be the one to tell me.

Which means I have to listen to a giant speech.

". . . a good time to reflect on the misery that all this monster nonsense of yours has caused," Dad says in his important-politician voice. "A chance for you to consider an attitude adjustment. Is that clear, Desmond?"

I nod as I always do at Dad's talks, wondering if I'll ever figure out what "taking stock of yourself" truly means. And for the billionth time, I wonder why the way his mustache moves when he speaks annoys me.

I see Dad's mouth continue to make shapes, and I hear sounds, but I'm not listening anymore. Because whenever Dad starts a speech with "Son, this is an opportunity . . . ," I just know things are about to get bad.

10 OH, IT'S BAD

Yep, I'm being forced to participate in extracurricular activities.

You could be a space alien from a galaxy light-years away and know just by the sound of those two words that it's something you don't want to do.

Only teachers invent phrases like "extracurricular activities." It's their tricky way of hiding the truth.

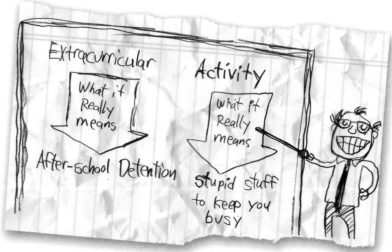

And believe it or not, there are kids who volunteer for this stuff. They actually *like* extracurricular activities. And they join many. This, of course, is where all teachers and dentists come from.

So now I'm signed up for three extracurricular activities. The only ones that had openings: A/V club. Newspaper club. And the worst . . . drama club.

Even the chess club kids torture the drama club kids.

"Your mother talked the school into giving you three more chances with these clubs, Desmond," Dad says sternly. "But this should keep you out of trouble, son," Dad continues confidently.

"You obviously have too much time on your hands. And idle hands are the devil's workshop."

IDOL HANDS

Add that to the list of junk Dad says that makes no sense.

So tomorrow is my first day of A/V club. And I want to make a good first impression. I've already picked out what I'm going to wear . . .

11 THE PHANTOM OF THE A/V CLUB

It's only my fourth day of forced extracurricular activities, and already I'm the number-one outcast of the A/V club. Which is really low, because everyone in the A/V club is an outcast.

"A/V club" is short for "audio/visual club," or as everybody else calls it . . .

TEAM DINGUS

Basically, the A/V club is a bunch of guys standing around in the school audio/visual room arguing about the best way to connect the audio/visual equipment. What wires to use, what inputs are fastest, what's the best video file type . . . Guh! After about fifteen minutes of that, I'd rather be back listening to the blabber of Rachel's friends. At least those girls know the importance of underarm deodorant.

The one real job the A/V club has is to run the morning announcements school TV show.

First it's the flag salute, and then the day's breaking school news . . .

. . . and other important stuff like that.

The show always ends with something fun, like a fun song from the girls' chorus or a teacher's fun knock-knock joke . . .

Obviously, when I say "fun" I mean "really stupid."

The morning announcements show is always the same. Nobody in the A/V club ever tries to do anything new. They're all too busy high-fiving one another for connecting the equipment right. But I want to try something different. And I have an idea.

There's only one problem: Brent Dungler.

Brent is captain of the A/V club.

Brent has all the power.

Since I'm the new guy, Brent gave me the lowest job: wire wrapper. It's my job to wrap up all the microphone and video wires.

And then Brent yells at me for not wrapping them right.

He loves yelling at me about my amateurishly wrapped wire.

Especially if other people are watching.

Nothing goes on Cloverfield Memorial Junior High TV without Brent's say-so.

Brent is the guy in charge of pushing the buttons in the control room.

And the most important button is . . .

. . . the "LIVE" button.

When this button is pushed, the morning announcements show is sent to every homeroom in the school.

So like I said, Brent has all the power.

I want that job.

I want the magic finger-pushing power.

So I have to get Brent out of the way.

And I know just how . . .

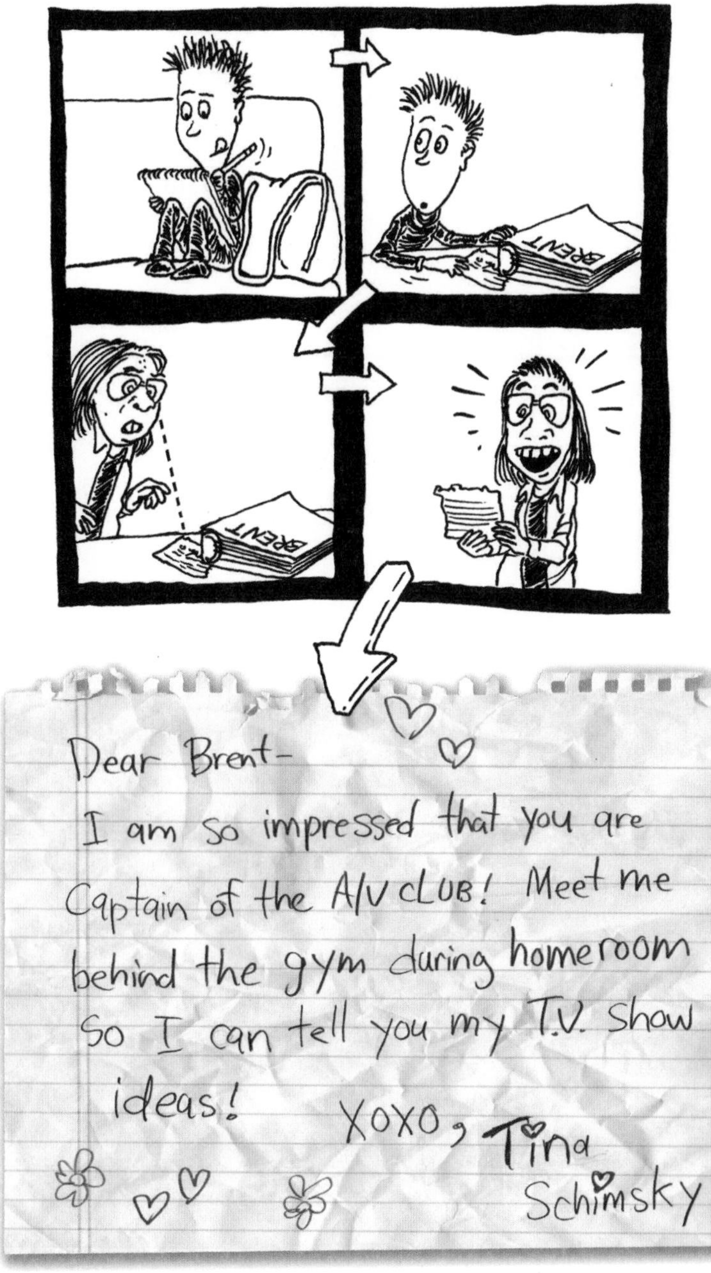
BRENT
BRENT
Dear Brent-
I am so impressed that you are
Captain of the A/V CLUB! Meet me
behind the gym during homeroom
so I can tell you my T.V. Show
ideas!
XOXO, Tina
Schimsky

Now, nobody in his right mind would ever think that the cutest girl in the sixth grade would have any interest in Brent Dungler.

Unless you're Brent Dungler. Giant-ego-head, captain-of-the-A/V-club Brent Dungler. He fell for the note instamatically.

So before Brent skips off to meet Tina Schimsky behind the gym, he turns the button-pushing job over to his second-in-command, Richard Lipnik.

But there's no way that Richard is ready for that kind of responsibility. Everybody knows that. And so ...

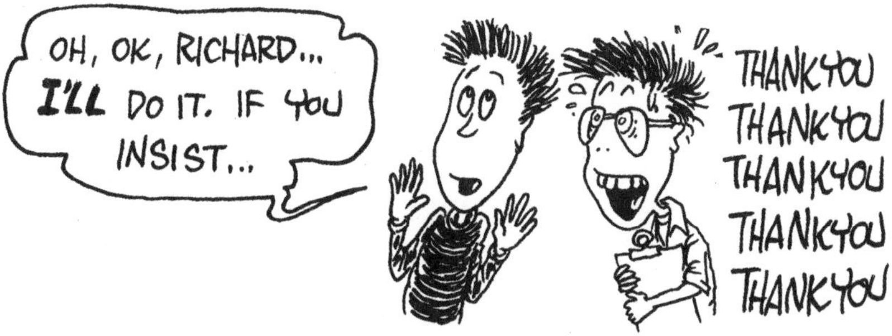
OH, OK, RICHARD...
I'LL DO IT. IF YOU INSIST...
THANKYOU THANKYOU THANKYOU THANKYOU THANKYOU

Yes! Let the magic begin!

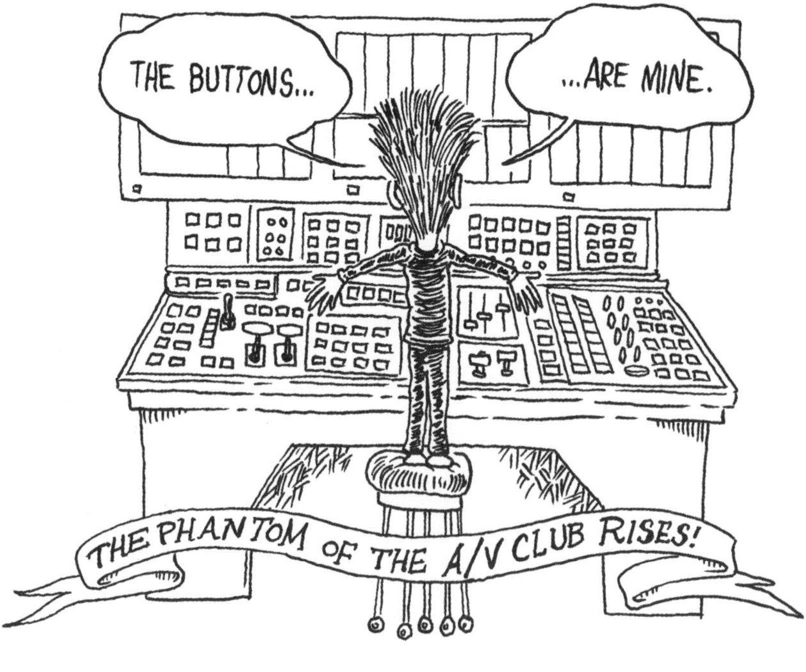
THE BUTTONS...
...ARE MINE.
THE PHANTOM OF THE A/V CLUB RISES!

Showtime arrives. Everybody stands up. Richard Lipnik holds his breath as I push the "LIVE" button. And right on cue . . .

. . . the flag salute goes off without a hitch.

Richard looks at me with relief and wipes pretend sweat from his forehead.

Then I switch cameras for the school news . . .

Sarah Ragguglio blabs on about changes to the girls' field hockey schedule and observing Keep Your Locker Sweet Week and other stuff nobody cares about.

The show is going perfectly.

It's perfectly dull, and everyone is perfectly bored.

Just like always. Richard Lipnik gives me the thumbs-up.

At last, it's time for the "fun" segment of the show!

My fingers fly over the buttons of the control room switchboard like I'm playing some giant nerd organ . . .

. . . and I go into full Phantom mode.

I press the final button to launch my "special presentation" . . .

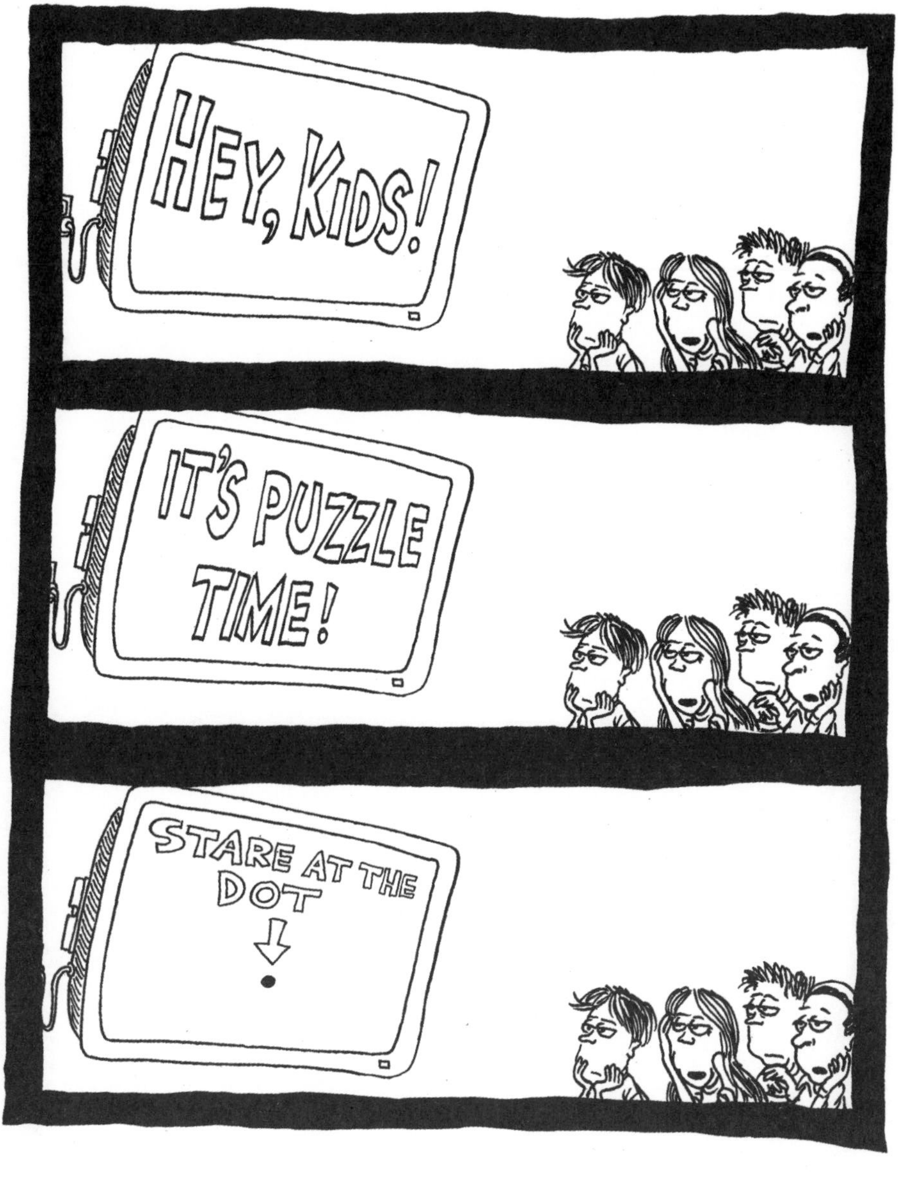
HEY, KIDS!
IT'S PUZZLE TIME!
STARE AT THE DOT

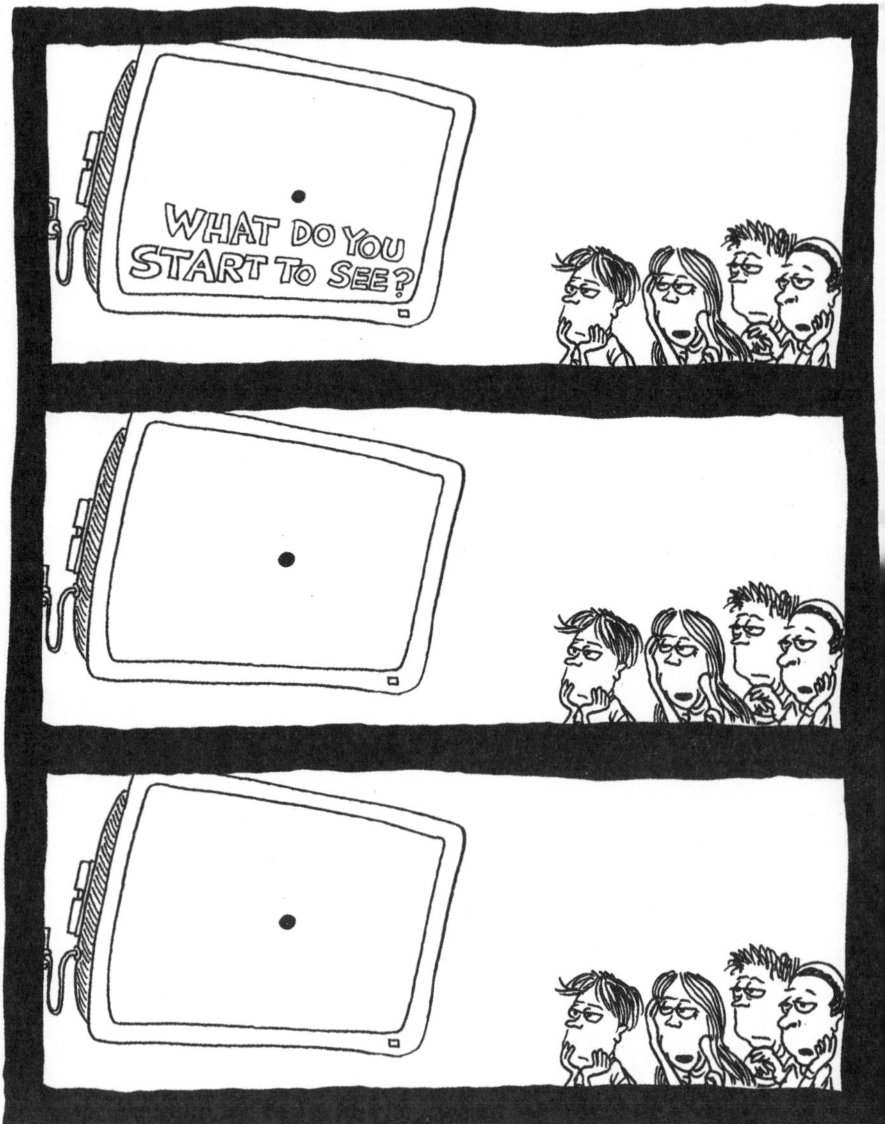
WHAT DO YOU START TO SEE?

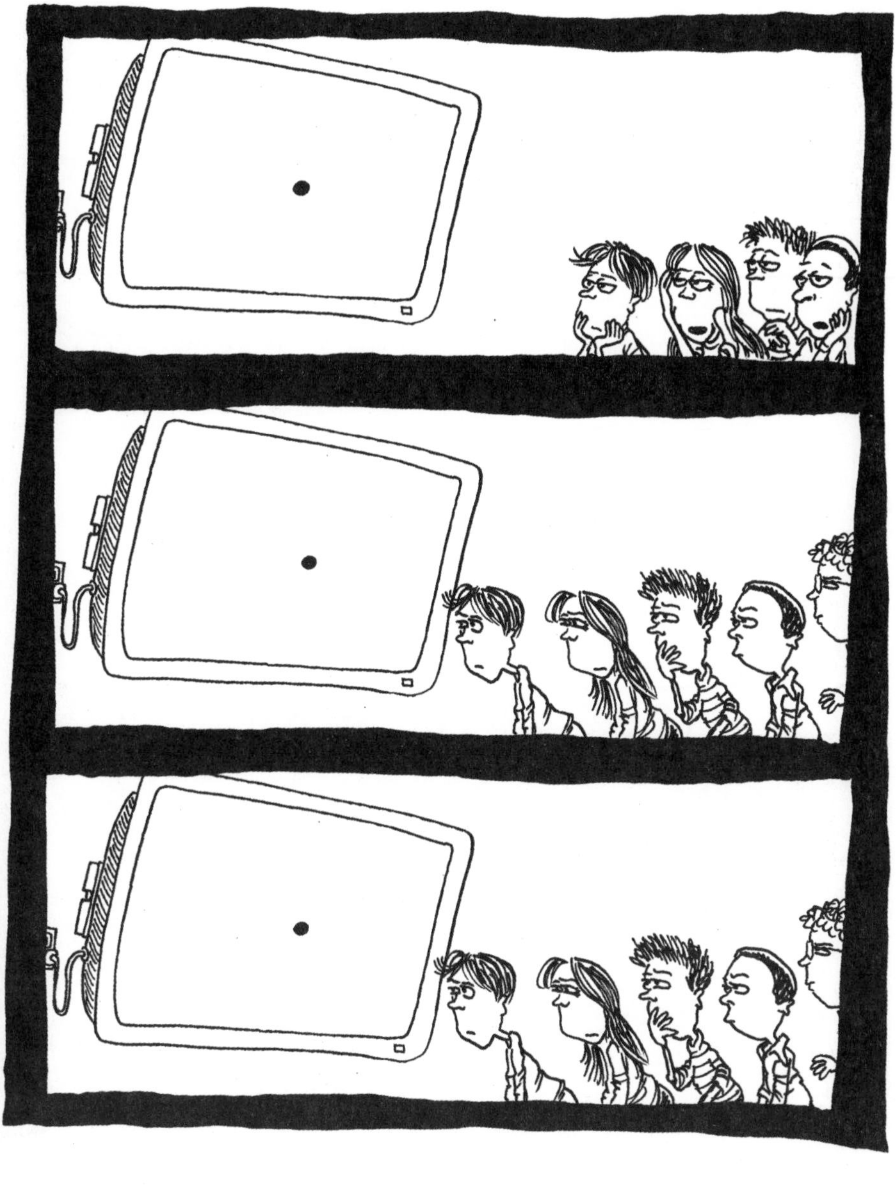

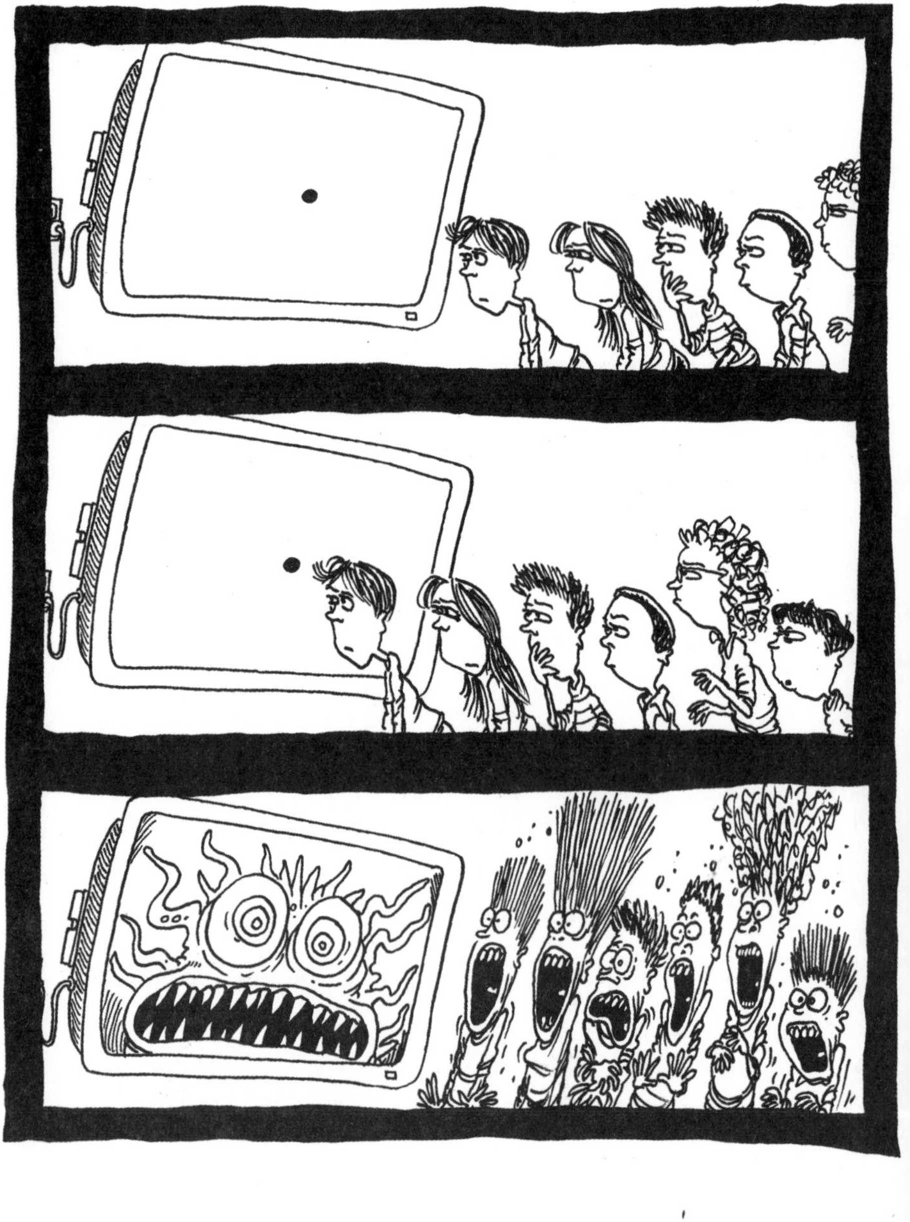

My first large-scale, mass-media, special-effects-monster-induced scream-a-thon!

The whole school . . . screaming!

At one of my creations!

To me, it's the sound of cheers.

And as I take my bow, I'm sure that somewhere out back behind the gym, Brent Dungler is still waiting patiently for Tina Schimsky to show up, and wondering what all the noise is.

As it turns out, not everybody appreciates my original programming . . .

CONTROL
ROOM--
A/V CLUB
ONLY!

12 ONE DOWN

In some weird way, I think Mr. Needles is the only person who really gets me.

He seems to be the only one who truly understands the awesomeness of my monster magic. How
else do you explain his hour-long lecture describing
everything I did in perfect detail? And that goofy, evil
smile on his face the whole time he's talking?

"Congratulations! You just got kicked out of the
A/V club! And now you're one step closer to getting
the boot from my school!"

OK, maybe that explains his creepy smile.

"Next up is newspaper club," he hisses, filling out an assignment slip. "Your second chance to prove you can adapt to a normal scholastic existence, which I obviously do not believe is possible."

Sometimes I think Mr. Needles was sentenced to life as a school disciplinarian for saying things like "normal scholastic existence."

"Report to room 417 after school," says Mr. Needles, waving the new assignment slip at me. "The Wickerstool twins, Jasper and Jessup, they run the show at the school newspaper. They'll tell you what to do."

I reach for the yellow piece of paper, but Mr. Needles holds tight, making me tug. He pulls me close to his face with a jerk.

"Your mother talked the school board into giving you three chances! They actually think you can change! But I'm about to prove them all wrong! **_Don't disappoint me!_**"

If it's possible for coffee breath to kill a person . . .

. . . Mr. Needles's should be registered as a lethal weapon.

I open my eyes (as if closing them could shut off my nose). I'm still alive. Mr. Needles finally lets go of the wrinkled slip and slowly leans back in his creaking chair, glaring at me the whole time.

Then he returns to his work, leaving me just sort of standing there.

"But this is your office, Mr. Needles. Don't you want to stay?"

"No, no, I mean, **you** should say 'may' instead of 'can' because—oh, never mind! Off with you!"

And he turns his head and waves me away, like a king sending a servant back to the castle kitchen.

A little tiny closet office with no windows must make you mad at the world. I'll have to remember that when I'm an adult.

13 THE CLOVERFIELD PLATYPUS

No, that's not the name of the monster that lurks in the swamp behind the baseball field. The Cloverfield Platypus is our school mascot. And it also happens to be the name of . . .

Yeah, pretty creative, right?

Like Mr. Needles told me, the *Cloverfield Platypus*

school newspaper is run by the Wickerstool twins, Jessup and Jasper. Which makes sense, because if there are any two guys who totally look like a couple of duckbill platypuses, it's them . . .

But I have to admit, I'm pretty excited about working on the school paper. What better way to show off my cartooning skills than a newspaper comic strip?

I talk Ricky into joining the paper with me, and we both walk in and present our first team effort, ready for publication.

I wonder if Jessup and Jasper would someday let me make a mold of their reaction faces, because . . .

. . . they would make sick monster masks.

"Great Jehoshaphat," sputters Jasper. "We can't print this stuff! You all must be dumber than stumps!"

The Wickerstool twins are from out of state and are always saying weird stuff like that, but don't let the goofy talk fool you. These guys are sharp and sneaky, and they know the dirt on everybody in school . . . and the whole town. They were born to be newspapermen.

IF WE PRINTED THIS, WE'D BE UP THE CRICK WITHOUT A PADDLE, SURE'S A YAM'S A TUBER!

WHAT'S A "YAM"?

I GUESS IT'S A "TUBER" ... WHATEVER THAT IS.

Jessup and Jasper may be smart newspaper guys, but they don't know crud about comic strips. Are they afraid of printing something that's too awesome?

"Look, you bozos already got an assignment, and it ain't a-making cartoons. Follow?"

It isn't what me and Ricky expected, but it's not like we have a choice. Like Jasper said, I can't screw this up. I don't want another strike.

Ricky wants to quit, but I agree to let him be the "action illustrator" for my report, and we mope off to the bleachers to cover the girls' soccer team.

Still, I can't help but wish we were heading over to the baseball field. I could easily write a thousand words about the swamp monster.

14 OF SOCCER AND SLOPPY JOES

OK, I take it back. There really is something worse than covering girls' soccer for the school newspaper.

Covering girls' soccer for the school newspaper under a wet blanket in the rain.

It's only a lunchtime practice, and the girls are taking turns missing free shots at the goal.

We're waiting for practice to end so we can interview Becca Krumpf, the star player . . . and when I say "star player," I mean "least bad."

Becca Krumpf mistakes Diana Simpson's face for the net.

Action Illustration by Ricky DiMarco

Ricky and I would be totally bummed if it weren't for our Sloppy Joe sandwiches and tater tots. And since the soccer action is about as exciting as watching paint dry, it isn't long before our minds start to wander . . .

Dang, I walked right into that!

"No, I mean, it's pretty obvious where the 'Sloppy' comes from. But did you ever wonder about the 'Joe' part?"

That gets us laughing and joking, and before you know it, this story almost writes itself . . .

THE FIRST SLOPPY JOE

Written by Desmond Pucket,
with Action Illustrations by Ricky DiMarco

I know when you think of a Sloppy Joe, you see a kaiser roll dripping with tomato sauce, onions, and loose pieces of hamburger meat.

But did you know that the first real Sloppy Joe was a person?

That's right!. Sloppy Joe Smeed was a janitor who worked in these very halls of our beloved Cloverfield Junior High, back around 1955.

He was called Sloppy Joe because he was
terrible at being a janitor.

Sloppy
Joe
Smeed

Whenever he went to clean up a mess, Sloppy
Joe made it worse! But nobody could fire him because
he was the nephew of the school principal. And this
made nobody madder than the school lunch ladies!

One day a kid threw up in the lunchroom kitchen, and Sloppy Joe Smeed was called. And just like always, he made it worse: instead of cleaning it up with his mop, he smeared puke all over the kitchen with his filthy tools.

The lunch ladies tried to grab his mop and do it right, but Sloppy Joe Smeed wouldn't let go, and there was a struggle. All around the kitchen they danced, the three lunch ladies swinging Sloppy Joe around by the wooden handle of the dirty mop.

meat grinder

And nobody was paying attention to how close they were all getting to the giant, churning meat grinder. Finally, Sloppy Joe Smeed pulled the mop from the lunch ladies, but he slipped on the wet floor and . . .

PLUNK!

. . . fell into the meat grinder. Then, with a *SPLASHH FERSHHHHLURP*, he was ground into tiny Smeed pieces and mixed in with the hamburger meat!

At first, the lunch ladies were shocked!

But then they smiled when they realized they had finally gotten rid of Sloppy Joe Smeed. So they added some tomato sauce, onions, and garlic to the grinder. Then the ladies smeared the new creation on rolls and tasted it.

With one big, yummy sound, they declared that was the best the janitor had made them feel in years! The Sloppy Joe sandwich was born!

Since that day (and until today), the special ingredient of the Sloppy Joe sandwich has been kept top secret by all who join the Coven of Lunch Ladies.

By the way, we had Sloppy Joes for school lunch today . . . Has anyone seen Janitor DeWicky?

THE END

Ricky and I are so wrapped up in our Sloppy Joe tale that we almost miss getting the real newspaper story.

But we do finally write and illustrate the soccer report and interview Becca Krumpf like we're supposed to and drop off the pages before deadline, and everything seems fine. Boring, but fine. And we forget all about Sloppy Joe Smeed and his sandwich.

Until the next day, when the whole school sees the story . . .

. . . splattered across the front page of *The Cloverfield Platypus News*!

15 STRIKE TWO

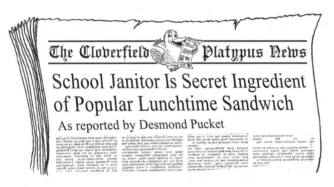

The Cloverfield Platypus News

School Janitor Is Secret Ingredient of Popular Lunchtime Sandwich

As reported by Desmond Pucket

Once again, I have the school screaming and gagging. Only this time, I did it without even trying!

RICKY, DID YOU SEE THIS?!

HOLY GUACAMOLE! I DON'T BELIEVE IT!

THEY CUT ALL OF MY ILLUSTRATIONS!

"Yeah, and lucky for you! Now I'm the only one who's gonna get in trouble!"

How did this happen?!

OK, let's backtrack: I wrote a lame-o story about the girls' soccer team, with lots of embellishments. ("Embellishments" is a fancy newspaper way of saying I lied about how good they are.) And Ricky did a bunch of action illustrations . . .

The MIGHTY PLATYPUS GIRLS' SOCCER

displaying awesome technique

Action Illustration by Ricky DiMarco

Then I put the finished soccer story in a folder . . .

. . . and dropped the pages off with Jessup Wickerstool.

Only, I must've given him the wrong folder—that's the only way I can explain the switcheroo!

And those goofball Wickerstools printed it!

Now, of course, I'm right back in Mr. Needles's office, trying to explain the mix-up.

Is it me, or does his little room get tighter every time I come in? Even the desk and chairs look like they're shrinking.

As I make my excuses, Mr. Needles slowly bounces in his squeaky chair and then holds up his hand for silence.

"Once again, Mr. Pucket, you exceed my expectations and create an even greater commotion than the last!"

I know Mr. Needles is supposed to be lecturing me, but again, he sure sounds like he's enjoying what I did.

"That Sloppy Joe story was a joke, Mr. Needles! I didn't mean for the Wickerstool twins to put it in the paper! Aren't editors supposed to watch out for these things?—"

"You can't expect the editors to read everything that goes into the newspaper, can you? It's the responsibility of the writer to make sure what's what!"

Mr. Needles smiles an ugly smile and leans forward on his shrinking desk.

I swear I see bits of yesterday's Sloppy Joe between his teeth.

"The point is this, Mr. Pucket: clever creative writing has no place in any newspaper. Only the cold, hard, uninteresting facts!

"But the deed is done. And so are *you*—with the school newspaper, boy! And since current events are the subject of the day, let me bring you up to speed . . ."

"One more strike and—but I won't say it! You still have time to make things right! You can turn things around! I have faith in you. But I also think pigs will fly!"

Mr. Needles laughs, but the smile doesn't make it to his eyes. And he hands me a new slip . . .

I leave Mr. Needles's office, and the same thing keeps turning over in my brain: One more chance to stay on the straight and narrow. One more chance to get this right, or Mr. Needles packs me off to Wood Hook Junior High and I miss the field trip to Crab Shell Pier and—

In my troubled daze I crash right into . . . Janitor DeWicky! He stares at me angrily.

"Thanks a heap, kid! You had my daughter freaking out, thinking she ate me for lunch yesterday!"

There's a sentence you don't hear every day.

"Ever wonder what happens to all the mixed vegetables that nobody eats? You're gonna find out, kid! I know which locker is yours."

I've got two strikes. And one more chance.

16 THE ME NOBODY SAW COMING

Ta-da! What do you think?

OK, here's the breakdown:

And don't forget the footwear!

You ever hear of "Goody Two-Shoes"? Well, this is it . . .

. . . penny loafers!

I even got rid of my . . .

. . . and replaced it with the very un-scary . . .

Because nothing says teacher's pet like a colorful notebook covered with dinggy zoo animals.

Yep, if you can't beat 'em, join 'em. And I'm joining 'em, full blast and in your face!

Of course, there are some who think my change is only skin-deep and not for real.

"Mr. Pucket, while a leopard might succeed in sponging off his spots, he will remain a leopard just the same," says a suspicious Mr. Needles.

Yes, that's right. I say things like "duly noted" now.

"I assure you I am in earnest, Mr. Needles," I continue, using my new mature-speak. "And I will take great pleasure in proving to you what an asset I can be to the entire Cloverfield scholastic system."

The look of shock on Mr. Needles's face when I stole his word "scholastic"

He'll probably never use it again!

And then there's Ricky.

Ricky and I have been number-one buds forever. We've never kept any secrets. Now I have to hit him with the new me, and it's going to pack a wallop.

"Hey, Desmond, you gotta see this machine I got! It makes fart sounds that come in eight different languages! Wait until you hear—"

Yep, it's hammer time.

This is going to be the hardest thing . . .

17 LATER, RICKY

"You look like you just stepped out of *Today's Modern Dorkus* magazine! Did somebody steal your clothes in gym?"

"Richard, if you will accompany me to the the-ater for drama club—"

"Is that a *zoo animal* notebook?!"

"Nobody is gonna believe you really changed *this* much!"

"That's where you're wrong, Richard. I *have* changed. And I have to make some other changes, too . . ."

I pull Ricky around the corner, push him against the lockers, and look right in his face.

"And you know how bad I want to go on the field trip! I've been waiting forever! I have to change everything! Not just the way I look, but my whole entire game!"

"I can't mess this up, Ricky! Mr. Needles connects you with the old me! I've got to make him think I'm totally serious! Then, once he backs off and we go to Crab Shell Pier, we can be friends again!"

"Whatever, dude! I won't screw it up for you, Desmond. I'm done. Before and after Crab Shell Pier."

A crumpled piece of paper falls out of Ricky's pocket as he walks off.

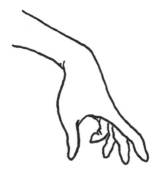

A Ricky cartoon.

Probably the last one I'll see for a long time.

Hard.

Hard hurts.

I hope this is worth it.

18 GOBSMACKED BY THE DRAMA CLUB

"Let's all give a big hi-dee-ho welcome to the drama club's newest member, Desmond Pucket!"

I hope not.

I make a small wave from my seat in the back of the theater . . .

. . . and the Drammies all turn to look at me, clapping politely.

"Aw, c'mon, Desmond!" booms Mr. Bramfield. "You can do better than that!"

Ugh. "Brammie's Drammies." That's even worse. I hope they don't make us wear T-shirts that say that.

Mr. Bramfield bounces on one foot, waving enthusiastically for me to stand.

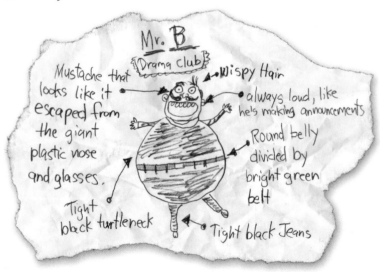

"Why don't you get up and tell the gang why you joined the drama club?"

I'm starting to wish Mr. Needles *had* kicked me out of school. I rise from my seat and . . .

"No, Desmond, up here, where we can see you!" Mr. B says, pointing to the space next to him.

In front of everybody.

Some kids snicker as I walk to the front. Mr. Bramfield must've taken advanced college courses in child humiliation.

My hand is in my pocket and I can feel a pair of monster teeth, a leftover from the old me . . .

For a second I think about popping them in my mouth, lunging at Mr. B, and scaring my way out of this. So easy . . .

But I remember the mission. *Crab Shell Pier—must stay focused.* I let go of the fangs and turn to face the audience.

And then I see her. In the third row. Is she actually glowing?

Tina Schimsky. The cutest girl in the sixth grade. Tina Schimsky is in the drama club.

I have no idea what I say next, because my brain is suddenly off in a daydream, just like in one of those corny old musicals my mom always watches.

The brick walls and curtains melt away, and . . . Tina and I dance off together . . .

. . . right into a sunset shot of Crab Shell Pier . . .

. . . to the very tippy-top of the Mountain Full of Monsters ride and—

I shake the goofy fantasy out of my head. The kids are all laughing, including Tina, who whispers something to Sheila Cutter.

"Like us all, you want to drink deeply of the elixir that is musical theater!"

Not exactly what I was going to say, but . . .

"And you'll all be happy to know," continues Mr. B, "that I've already picked this year's musical!"

Mr. Bramfield is famous for picking the lamest of lame-o musicals,

. . . and he's a sucker for a theme show.

He dances row to row, handing out scripts.

"Tryouts start tomorrow, gang! Anyone who doesn't get a part is still on the stage crew or lighting! There's always something for everyone to do!"

I look at the script.

Guh! I just know that, somewhere, Mr. Needles is laughing his butt off.

And waiting for me to fail again.

19 DESMOND THE STRIPED AND COLORFUL

It's been two weeks since I made the transformation to supergalactic nerdboy, and it's all going according to plan. Everybody likes the new me, which really makes me wonder . . .

WHAT WAS SO BAD ABOUT THE OLD ME?

Mom loves buying clothes for the new me.

I used to be a basic-black guy (a good effects man is always ready to blend into the shadows), but now I'm all about bright oranges and reds and lime green. I didn't even know they made boys' pants in those colors! And striped shirts of every kind. Some days I go to school looking like a giant dish of birthday cake ice cream with a side order of jelly beans.

Dad is really happy to see the change in me, too.

He is so encouraged by my turning to the dweeb side that he leaves a couple brochures on my bed . . .

Speaking of acting, Mr. Bramfield likes the dorky Desmond so much that he makes me captain of Brammie's Drammies.

Putting my special-effects expertise to good use, I rewire the theater lights, and now we can make it rain or snow or flash lightning onstage with a flick of a button. Mr. B even gives me a small part in the circus musical. My big scene is selling a balloon to the female lead, Tina Schimsky.

So life is good right now. There are only two problems: Ricky and Mr. Needles.

My friendship with Ricky is the one thing I really miss! Whenever I have a cool new idea or draw an awesome cartoon, I have nobody to show it to. Ricky is the one person who really gets me.

I hate ignoring Ricky, but Mr. Needles is watching me so closely that I can't make any mistakes.

I'VE GOT MY EYES ON YOU, PUCKET...

Now that things are going so good with the drama club, it's like Mr. Needles is watching from around every corner, waiting for the tiniest slip-up so he can nail me.

Every day I get one step closer to the field trip to Crab Shell Pier and the Mountain Full of Monsters ride! I just have to hold on a little longer. I'm so close! Everything is working perfectly!

So of course, that's when things start going wrong . . .

20 THE SLIMY SETUP

This could be trouble . . .

Somebody slimed Tina Schimsky.

I look at Tina standing center stage, every bit of her covered in green, drippy goop. Her mouth is frozen in a silent scream. Her eyes are half rolling up into her lids.

Tina Schimsky even makes Gak look good!

I'm not sure what that means, but it sounds like a compliment.

"Thanks! But it wasn't me this time, Mr. B! I don't do that stuff anymore! I'm captain of Brammie's Drammies! I'm clean! I swear! I didn't—"

Just then, a high-pitched scream shatters our eardrums. That can only be Sheila Cutter. Even though Sheila pretty much screams all the time, this one sounds especially horrified.

Sheila bolts out from behind the curtains and onto the stage, covered in cottony webs and hundreds of fake spiders.

She's so wildly out of control, flinging her arms and spinning and knocking over set pieces, that she crashes right into Tina Schimsky. They both end up on the stage floor, a mass of gloppy slime, tangled webs, and plastic creepy-crawlers . . .

. . . and much screaming.

All of a sudden, another bucket of purple goo dumps . .

. . . right onto Mr. Bramfield's comb-over, and he joins in the girls' screaming.

As the slime-drenched Mr. B reaches out to grab me, I back away and trip . . .

. . . falling off the stage and into the orchestra pit!

Thankfully, I land on the softness of Thomas Proll, the tuba player. But my fall sets off a chain reaction of music stands crashing into other music stands. Sheet music flies everywhere. Metal and wood instruments clatter across the floor.

As I run from the theater, I think about what Mr. B just said . . .

Somebody is trying to make the whole drama club think I want to sabotage the musical! But who would set me up?

Then I remember the other word Mr. B said earlier: "**prankster.**"

And there's only one prankster I can think of who would want to see me get kicked out of the drama club . . .

21 ATTACK OF THE RICKY

I knew that atomic-wedgie training would come in handy one day . . .

I just never thought I'd be using it on my ex-best friend.

"What the—!" sputters Ricky. "First you say you can't be seen near me, and next thing you're pulling my underwear over my head!"

"You set me up by pulling all those pranks on the drama club just to get me kicked out!"

"What are you talking about, dipstick?!"

"I know it was you," I sputter. "Who else knows I use that brand of high-gloss superstick spider webs?"

"You're combing your hair too tight, Pucket! It's affecting your brain!"

I notice a crowd is forming around us—and it's growing. I snap right back at Ricky: "Yeah, well, at least I wash and comb *my* hair!"

OK, you're definitely not dealing with master insulters here. We're in way over our heads. But the crowd doesn't care. And it isn't long before Scott Seltzer yells . . .

. . . and the mob joins in.

Ricky suddenly dives . . .

. . . knocking me to the ground.

We roll around, swinging wildly at each other, neither of us getting any shots in.

The truth is out: Ricky and I stink at insulting **and** fighting. But we try to put on a good show.

Suddenly, the crowd scatters . . .

. . . and we're lifted up by a strong grip on our collars.

"Mr. Bramfield, I swear I didn't—"

"Mr. Pucket, I am prepared to take you at your word and give you another chance at the drama club . . ."

"And since I suspect your friend here may have had a hand in the recent theater slimings, I think he will be a nice addition to our stage crew . . . *or* face Mr. Needles!"

Ricky and I frown at each other. Mr. B is forcing us to work together in the drama club!

Well, at least now I can keep an eye on my **ex**-best friend. And if he tries any funny stuff, I'll catch him in the act!

22 LAST CHANCE

I'm an outcast in the drama club. I can feel my last chance to go on the class field trip to Crab Shell Pier slipping away.

Everybody blames me for yesterday's slime-a-thon, and now that Ricky has been forced into the stage crew, they all expect me and him to team up.

So now I have to work twice as hard to convince them all I'm still captain of Brammie's Drammies!

So I bake cookies for the drama club fundraiser.

I work late painting backdrops. I help Mrs. DeNeen with the costumes, listening to her endless stories about her three poodles.

I even volunteer to fold and staple the programs, the worst drama club job of all.

And most importantly, I steer clear of Ricky.

If he's on one side of the room, I'm on the other. Slowly but surely, I'm winning back the trust of the drama club.

And then, just as suddenly, it starts happening again.

Little things at first . . .

Then it gets worse: itching powder in the costumes, stink bombs in the dressing rooms, Mr. Bramfield's special stash of wintergreen breath mints switched out for garlic flavor . . .

(And Mr. Bramfield likes to get right up in your kitchen when he talks, so this last thing is pretty much the worst.)

Once again, everybody thinks it's me. The Drammies all start giving me the silent treatment, and Mr. Bramfield, sick of all the interruptions, threatens to report me to Mr. Needles.

MR. B, I SWEAR IT'S NOT ME! JUST GIVE ME A CHANCE TO PROVE IT!

"OK, Desmond, you have twenty-four hours to prove all these shenanigans are not your doing! Our show opens in a few days!"

WE HAVE NO MORE TIME FOR SUCH TOMFOOLERY!

OK, so Mr. B has given me a day to clear myself. And I'm going to use it. I'm going to get the creep who's trying to frame me.

I smell a Ricky rat. And it's time to set a trap . . .

23 TRAPPING THE RAT

I'm getting tired.

I've been crouching near the stage in the shadows of the curtains for hours, waiting for something to happen. To pass the time, I imagine myself on the Mountain Full of Monsters ride with Tina Schimsky.

Of course, the main thing keeping me here is the big payoff . . .

I smile thinking about Ricky standing in front of Mr. B and Mr. Needles, confessing and being totally humiliated that his trick to get me kicked out of drama club didn't work. And then suddenly . . .

. . . I hear a noise in the hallway!

This is it! The dummy has returned to the scene of the crime! What a dope! I ready myself as the stage door starts to open . . .

"Got ya!"

OK, so it's not the perfect net . . .

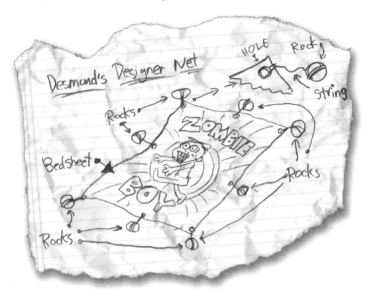

I made it out of one of my old Zombie Boy bed-sheets, but it did the trick! I caught a rat, just like I thought!

I can see the rat is totally shocked and confused as he fights with the bedsheet net. I run over and grab the sheet to pull it off, because I can't wait to see the look on Ricky's face . . .

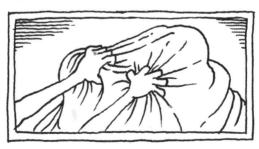

"Jessup and Jasper!" I gasp. "What's going on?! I don't get it! Are you the guys who've been trying to set me up?"

"Yep, it was us, all right," says Jasper. "Guess it's time to come clean . . ."

24 THE STORY OF JASPER AND JESSUP

"I have something you really need to see!"

I pass Mr. Needles the hand-drawn pages I've just completed after listening to Jessup and Jasper's story.

"What is this, boy?" he snarls, taking the papers. "Comics? I have no time for this nonsense!"

"No, sir! Well, yes, it's comics—but it's also a confession!"

Mr. Needles growls and begins reading the crumpled pages.

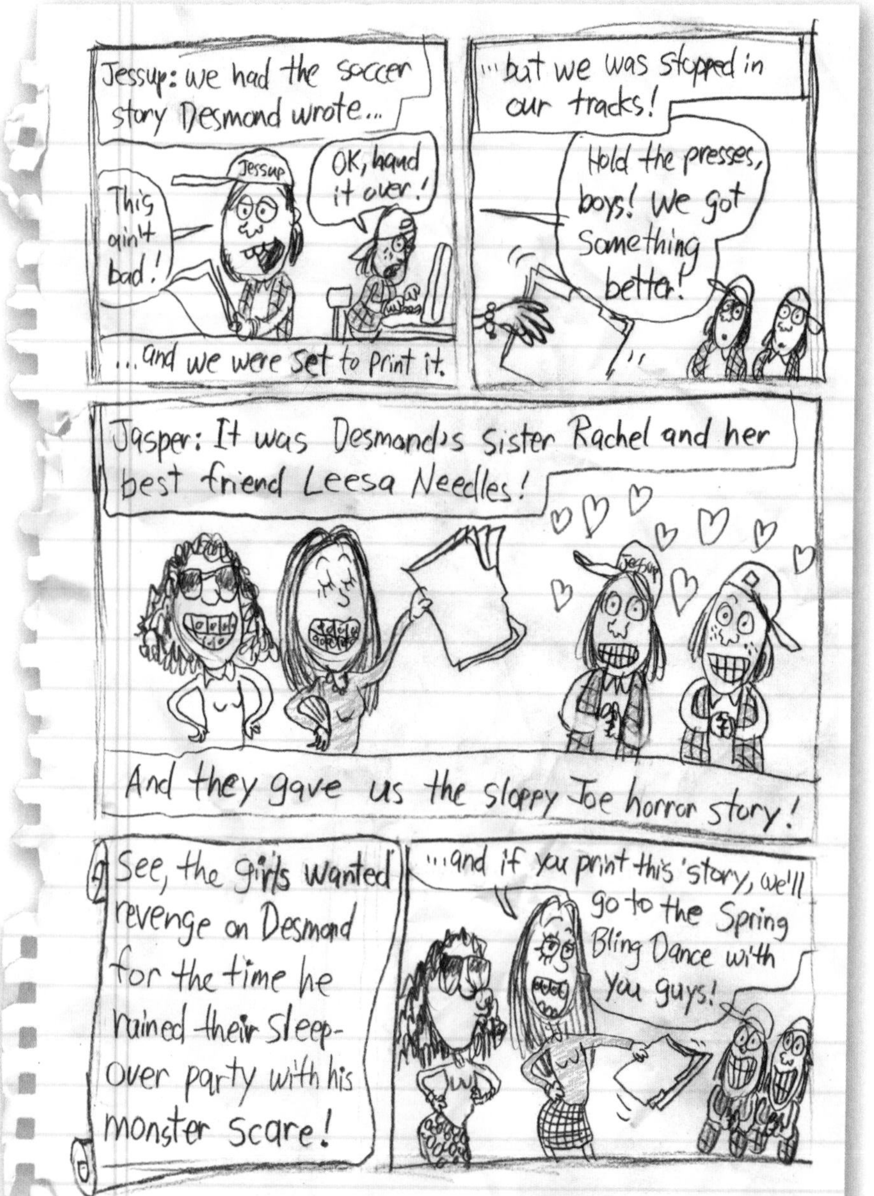
Jessup: we had the soccer story Desmond wrote...
This ain't bad!
Jessup
OK, hand it over!
...and we were set to print it.
...but we was stopped in our tracks!
Hold the presses, boys! We got something better!
Jasper: It was Desmond's sister Rachel and her best friend Leesa Needles!
Jessup
And they gave us the sloppy Joe horror story!
See, the girls wanted revenge on Desmond for the time he ruined their sleep-over party with his monster scare!
...and if you print this 'story,' we'll go to the Spring Bling Dance with you guys!

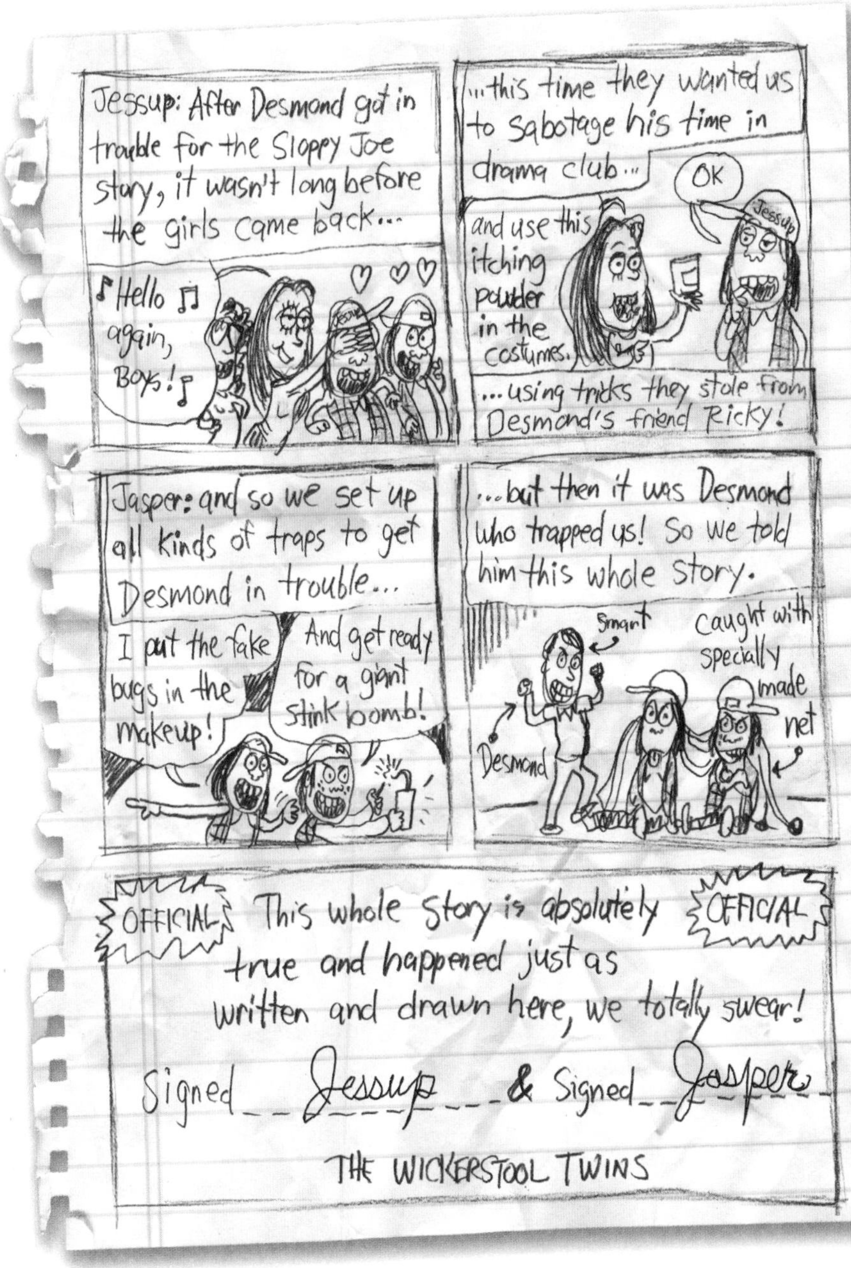

Jessup: After Desmond got in trouble for the Sloppy Joe story, it wasn't long before the girls came back...
Hello again, Boys!
...this time they wanted us to sabotage his time in drama club...
OK
Jessup
and use this itching powder in the costumes.
...using tricks they stole from Desmond's friend Ricky!
Jasper: and so we set up all kinds of traps to get Desmond in trouble...
I put the fake bugs in the makeup!
And get ready for a giant stink bomb!
...but then it was Desmond who trapped us! So we told him this whole story.
Smart
Desmond
caught with specially made net
OFFICIAL
OFFICIAL
This whole story is absolutely true and happened just as written and drawn here, we totally swear!
Signed Jessup & Signed Jasper
THE WICKERSTOOL TWINS

Mr. Needles just stands there staring at the pages, and I wait for him to react.

"You have some imagination, Pucket. That sure is an interesting story," he says finally.

"But you're too late, sir," he says, sprinkling the shredded bits of paper in front of my face. "Your future has already been decided. I just had a secret meeting with the school board."

"But, Mr. Needles, I didn't—"

He holds up his hand and continues.

"I couldn't get you booted out of Cloverfield, but the board agrees that I have enough evidence to keep you from going on the field trip to Crab Shell Pier.

"But don't worry, Pucket. I'm sure your friends will all take pictures of what you're missing!"

25 GAME OVER

I stand there in shock, rooted to the spot.

That's it. I'm done. Toast. Game over.

Everything I did to change myself and clean up my act and stop scaring people was for nothing. All the work, the extracurricular activities, staying away from Ricky, wearing brightly colored shirts and sensible shoes! All for nada! Mr. Needles went ahead and did what he wanted to do anyway! He cut me from the trip to Crab Shell Pier!

I still can't move when the Wickerstool twins walk over.

"I told him," I say. "I told him, but he didn't care. He didn't care because he expects me to be this way! I think everybody expects me to be this way!"

As usual, Jessup looks confused.

"Expects you to be what way?"

I walk to my locker. I fling the door open and . . .

. . . a mess of day-old mixed vegetables comes tumbling out. I laugh to myself. Looks like Janitor DeWicky has been here. Well, he's in for a big surprise, too!

I reach deep inside my locker . . .

"You lost your mind, boy? What gives?" asks Jasper.

I turn to the Wickerstool twins.

"Nothing's wrong! It's all good! It's perfect, in fact," I say. "But we have to hurry! Tomorrow is opening night of the musical, and everyone will be there! I need your help!"

"What did you have in mind, son?" Jasper asks.

"Nothing too wacky, Desmond!"

"Don't worry, Jasper," I say. "The sleepover party was great, but this for sure will be my ultimate super-epic masterpiece!"

DESMOND'S BACK, BOYS...

...AND WE'RE GONNA MAKE SOME MONSTER MAGIC!

But first, there's a big wrong that I have to make right . . .

26 THE SORRY

He should be coming by soon.

He used to always come this way. A shortcut to school, through Mrs. Stravalli's hedges.

All right, one down. I'll try again in Mrs. Trench's science class.

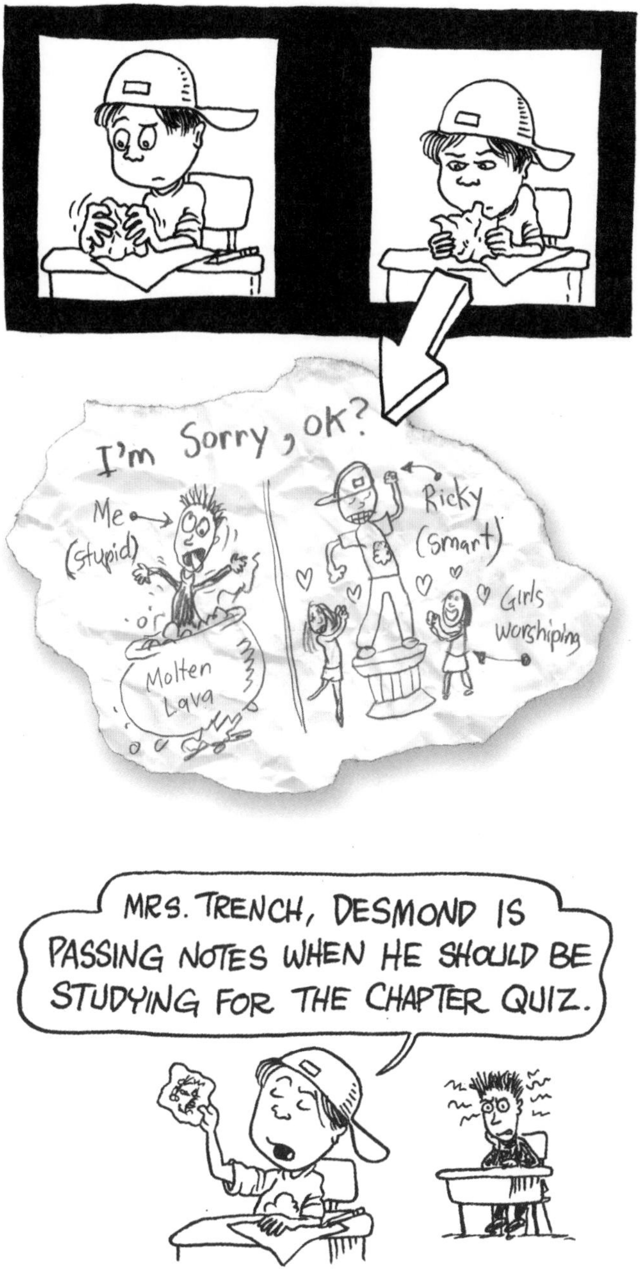
I'm Sorry, ok?
Me
(stupid)
or
Molten Lava
Ricky
(smart)
Girls worshiping
MRS. TRENCH, DESMOND IS PASSING NOTES WHEN HE SHOULD BE STUDYING FOR THE CHAPTER QUIZ.

OK, if this doesn't work,

I give up . . .

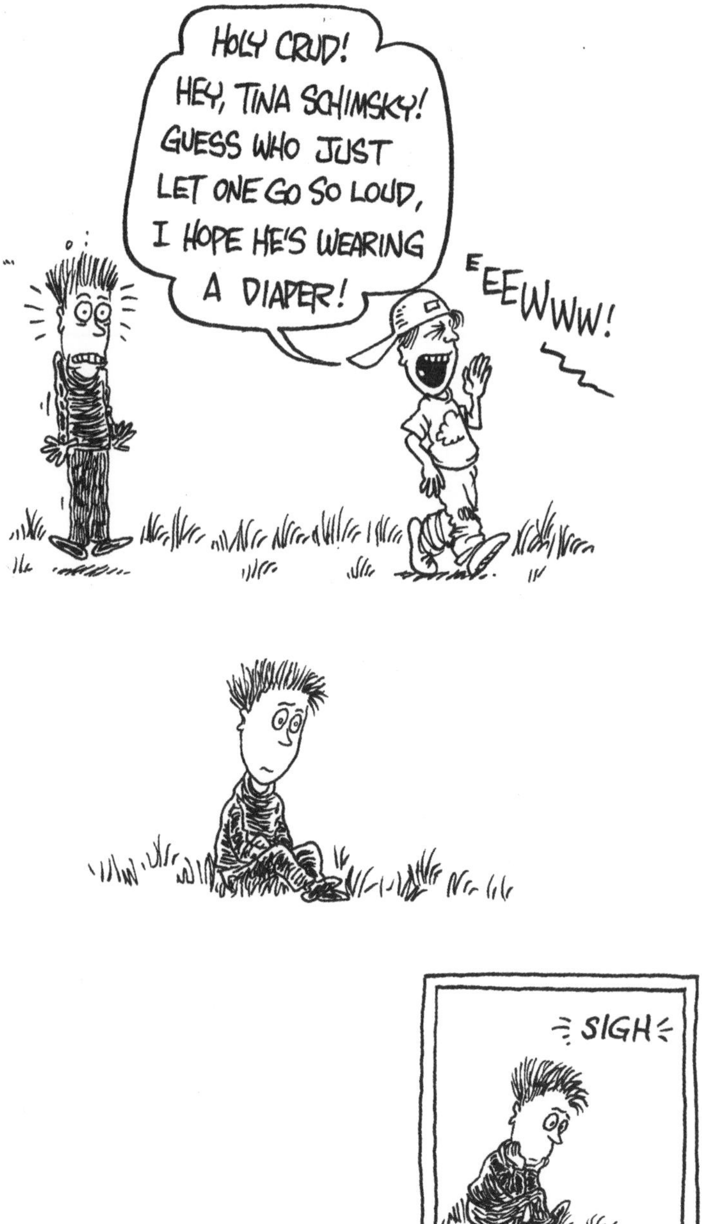
HOLY CRUD! HEY, TINA SCHIMSKY! GUESS WHO JUST LET ONE GO SO LOUD, I HOPE HE'S WEARING A DIAPER!
EEEWWW!
SIGH

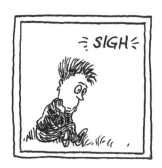

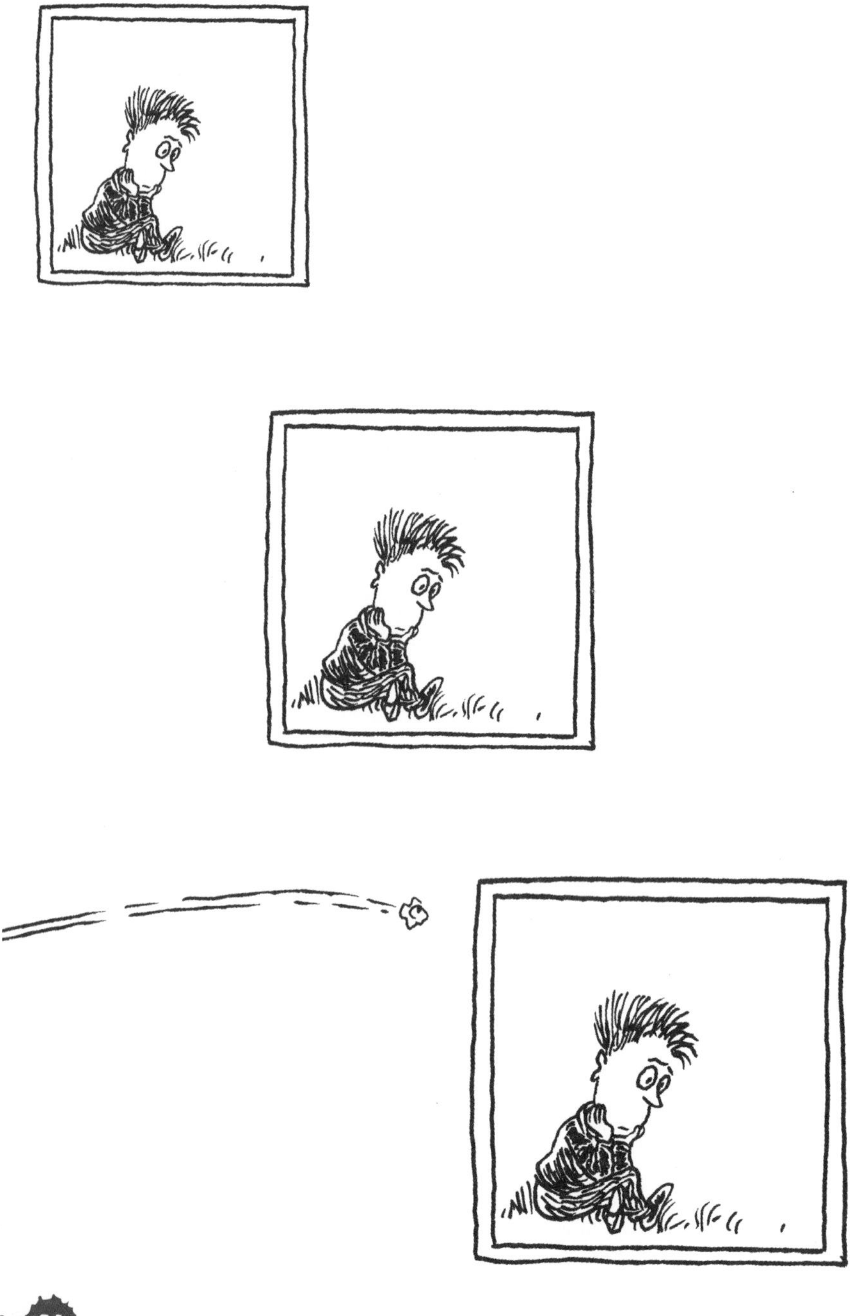

OK.

Ricky (cool)

Desmond (weird)

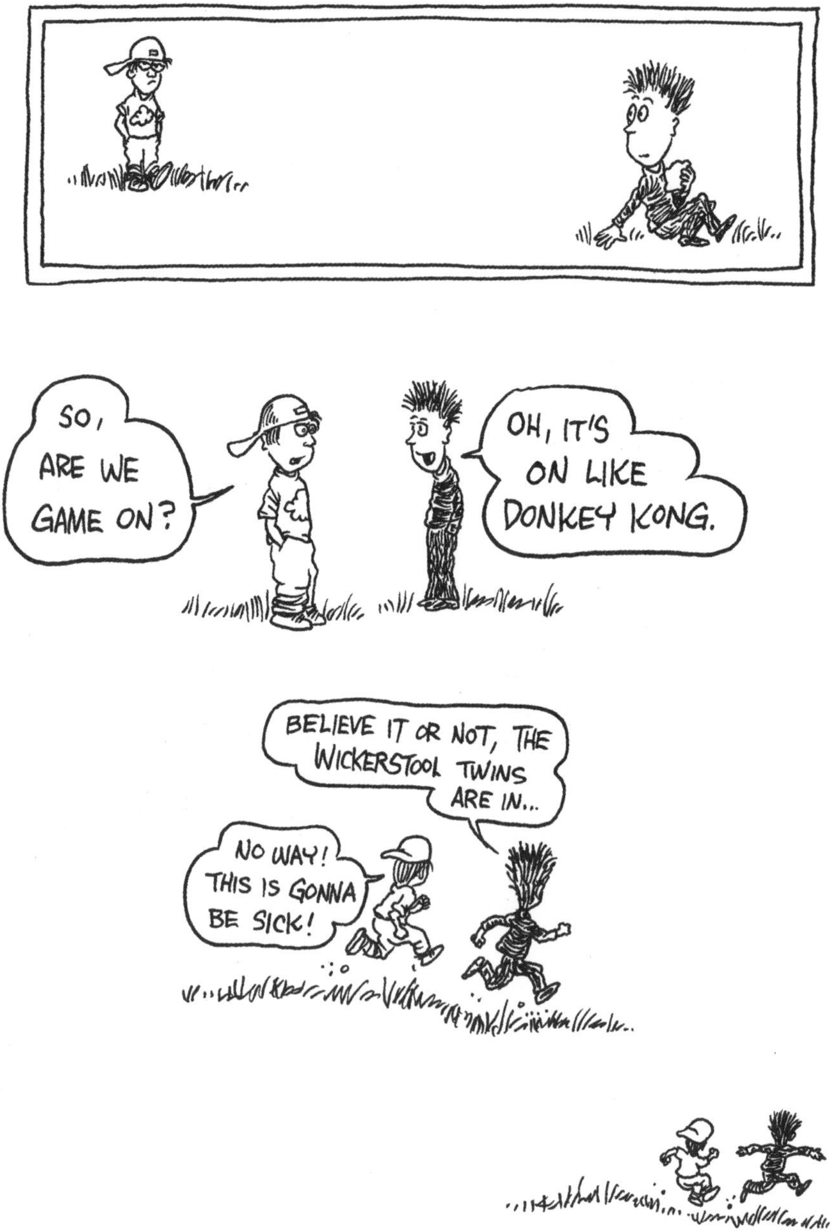
SO, ARE WE GAME ON?
OH, IT'S ON LIKE DONKEY KONG.
BELIEVE IT OR NOT, THE WICKERSTOOL TWINS ARE IN...
NO WAY! THIS IS GONNA BE SICK!

27 OPENING NIGHT

It's a full house.

Everybody's here, just like I thought.

"Desmond Pucket!" Mr. Bramfield whisper-shouts. "Get away from that curtain! Actors don't peek out at the audience!"

"Well, don't wait until the last minute! You're already on borrowed time, son!"

Mr. B knows I've been kicked off the class field trip, but he decided to let me stay in the show. He's a pretty good egg. And he's got the body shape to prove it.

They say it's totally normal to be nervous before a show. To have butterflies in your stomach.

Yeah, I'm nervous all right, but it's not because I'm afraid of forgetting my lines. I play the balloon vendor, and I only have one . . .

But my line is pretty important. It's in the final act, the last spoken line of the musical.

It also happens to be the cue to start my most *epic* monster magic production ever!

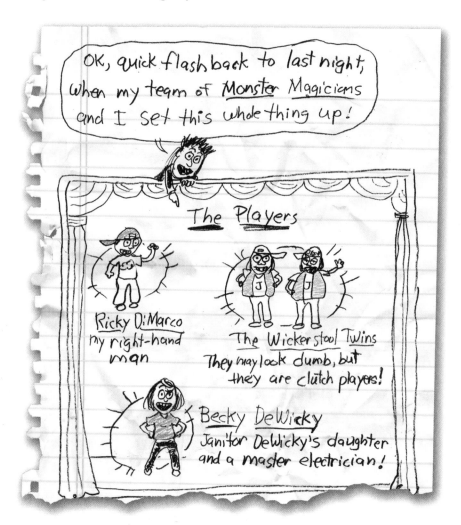

After the final dress rehearsal last night, we pretended to leave. Then we hid backstage and waited for everyone else to go. Once the last light clicked off and the door slammed shut, we sprang into action!

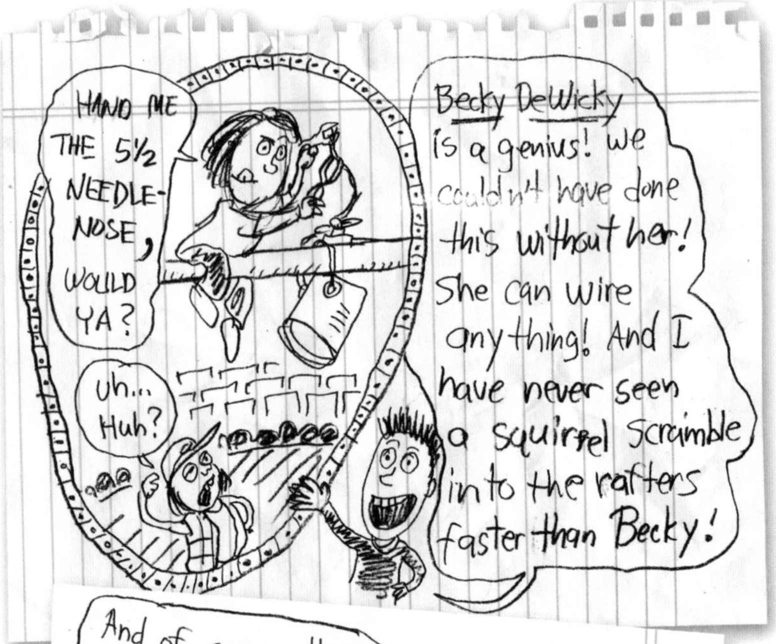

HAND ME THE 5½ NEEDLE-NOSE, WOULD YA?
Uh... Huh?
Becky DeWicky is a genius! We couldn't have done this without her! She can wire anything! And I have never seen a squirrel scramble into the rafters faster than Becky!

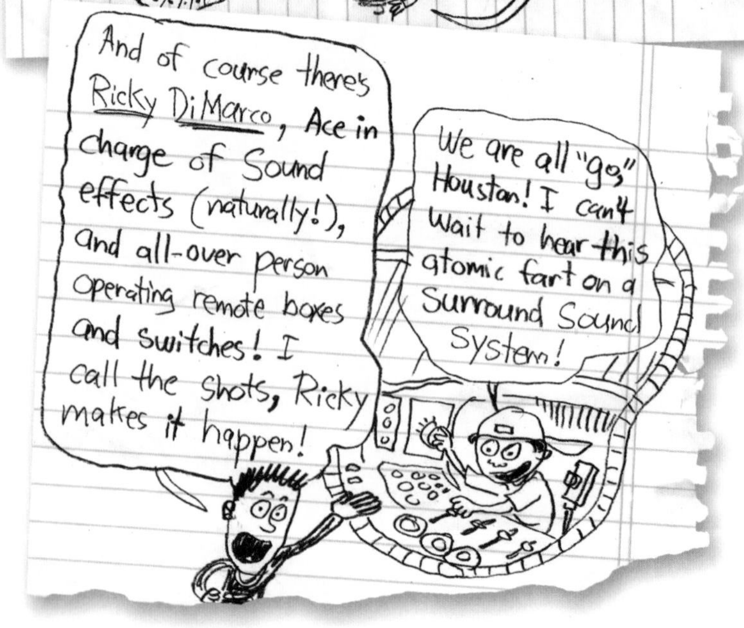

And of course there's Ricky DiMarco, Ace in charge of Sound effects (naturally!), and all-over person operating remote boxes and switches! I call the shots, Ricky makes it happen!
We are all "go," Houston! I can't wait to hear this atomic fart on a Surround Sound System!

We worked until 4 a.m., cutting, tying, running wires, hooking up switches, and setting lights. We didn't even have time to test anything. The first time we will see if everything works is during the show itself!

"Desmond Pucket! Hurry now! Hurry! Get into your costume! It's—"

"Yes, I know, Mr. B! I know—"

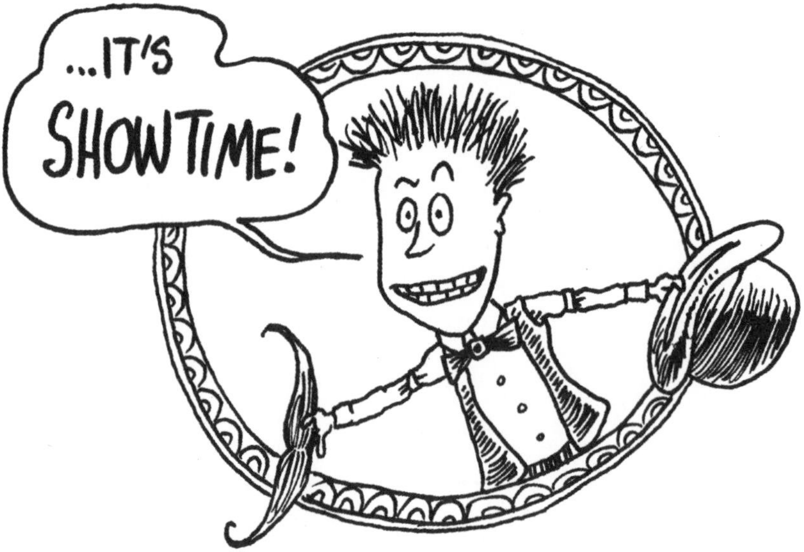
...IT'S SHOWTIME!

28 STAGE FRIGHT

One hour and forty-five minutes later, Mr. Bramfield's production of *Merry-Go-Musical: A Circus of Songs!* is almost over. The audience is packed with school officials and parents and teachers and kids and aunts and uncles and grandmas and grandpas, and they're all really, really . . .

. . . *bored.*

It's not that Mr. B picks boring shows to do. OK, yes, Mr. B always picks boring shows to do. But I'm sure those musicals were exciting when they were first written. Back in 1842. In any case, the audience is in a half-asleep stupor. And that's just how I want them. A bored audience is ripe for the fright!

Ulp. I'm starting to feel those pterodactyls again. "Desmond! Your cue! Get onstage, boy!"

It's Ricky, in my earpiece. Calling from up in the sound and lighting booth. Good ol' Ricky.

I walk onstage with my balloons and mustache. I can't see the audience because of the stage lights. And then I turn and see her. Tina Schimsky. Amazing in her costume and glowing in the bright beams! My heart is thumping in my ears.

Holy guacamole, she is so beautiful that I . . .

that I . . .

I don't believe it. My one line. I forgot my one, all-important line!

And that is how Mr. Bramfield steals my one line—and without even knowing it, signals the start of my most colossal monster magic show ever . . .

29 EPIC

Ricky kills the lights.

The entire theater goes pitch black.

In the darkness, Jasper darts onto the stage and hooks a rope to the harness on my back. Then he gives a tugging signal to Jessup, who pulls on the other end. A long sharp hiss is heard, and the stage fills with fog, spilling into the audience. Before anyone can react, fiendish red, green, and purple lights kick on, washing the entire fog-covered stage and the stunned actors.

Heavy metal music, punctuated by atomic farts, blares from gigantic speakers. (I would have gone with eerie organ music or a horror movie soundtrack, but the audio is Ricky's baby!) And I, the balloon man in my harness, hoisted into the air by Jessup, float over the entire scene. So far, so good!

I see Mr. Bramfield running around backstage in confusion, barking into his headset. The audience is starting to murmur and look around, wondering what's going on. Let's get this party started!

The dozen fifteen-foot giant waving monsters (donated by Jasper's friends at Frenggle Brothers Dodge and Toyota) inflate through the fog one by one and flutter over the shocked audience.

I think it's safe to say they're not bored anymore!

This is Becky's coolest invention! She wired cans of silly string to an old keyboard! Then she placed the cans in high strategic places all over the theater.

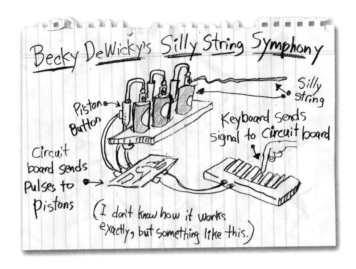

And when she hits different keys, different-colored cans of silly string squirt out over the audience!

I told you she was a genius!

And then the lightning and thunder effects flash and crash, which naturally means . . .

Although it's the simplest effect, rain is always the best. There's nothing adults hate worse than being wet. Have you ever seen a kid with an umbrella? Only adults. If you ever see a kid with an umbrella, you know it's because some adult made him carry it.

But even adults with umbrellas are no match for what comes next . . .

And on that command, the confetti cannons erupt . . .

. . . showering the audience with buckets of rubber snakes, plastic spiders, and fake cockroaches!

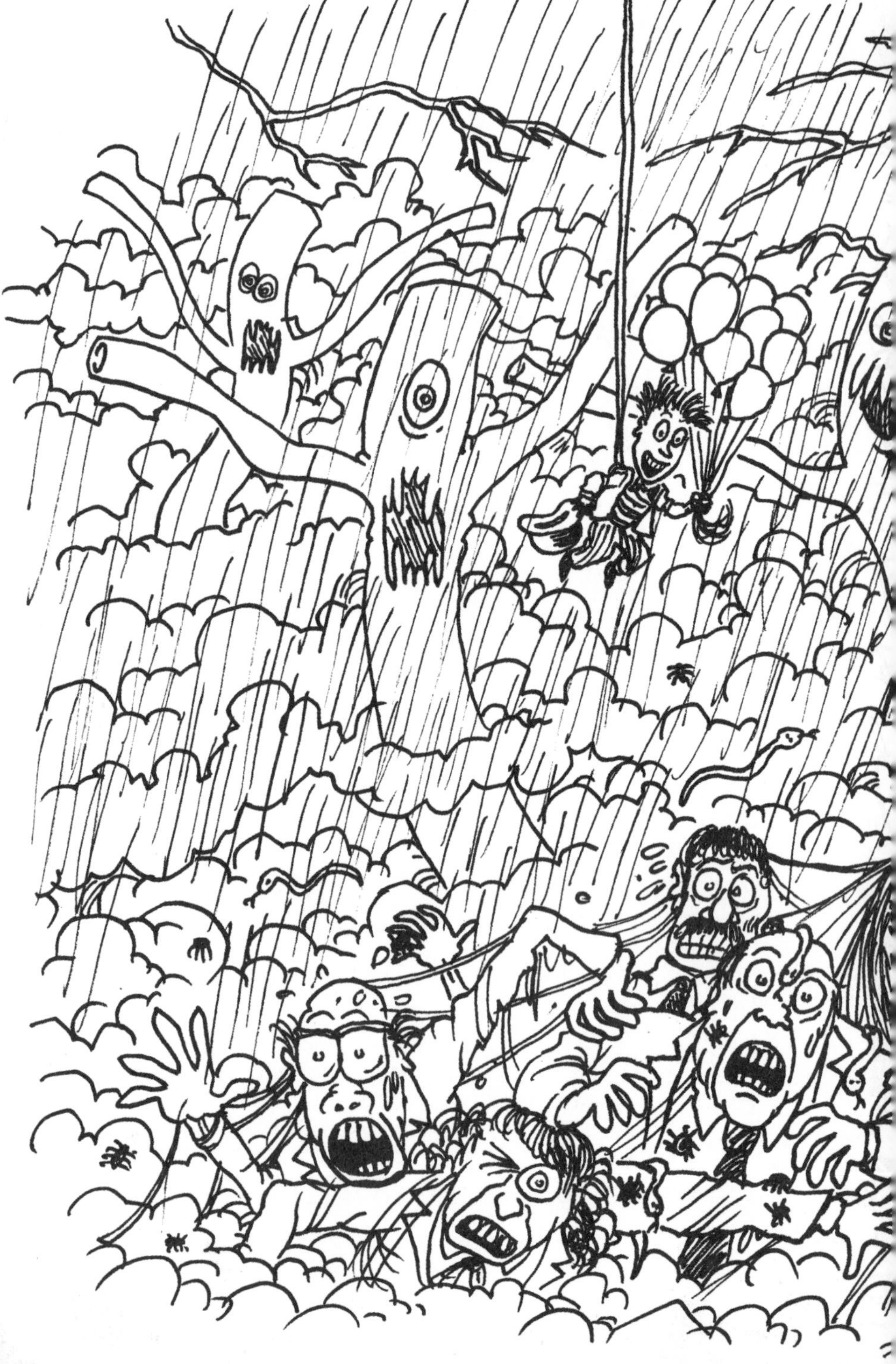

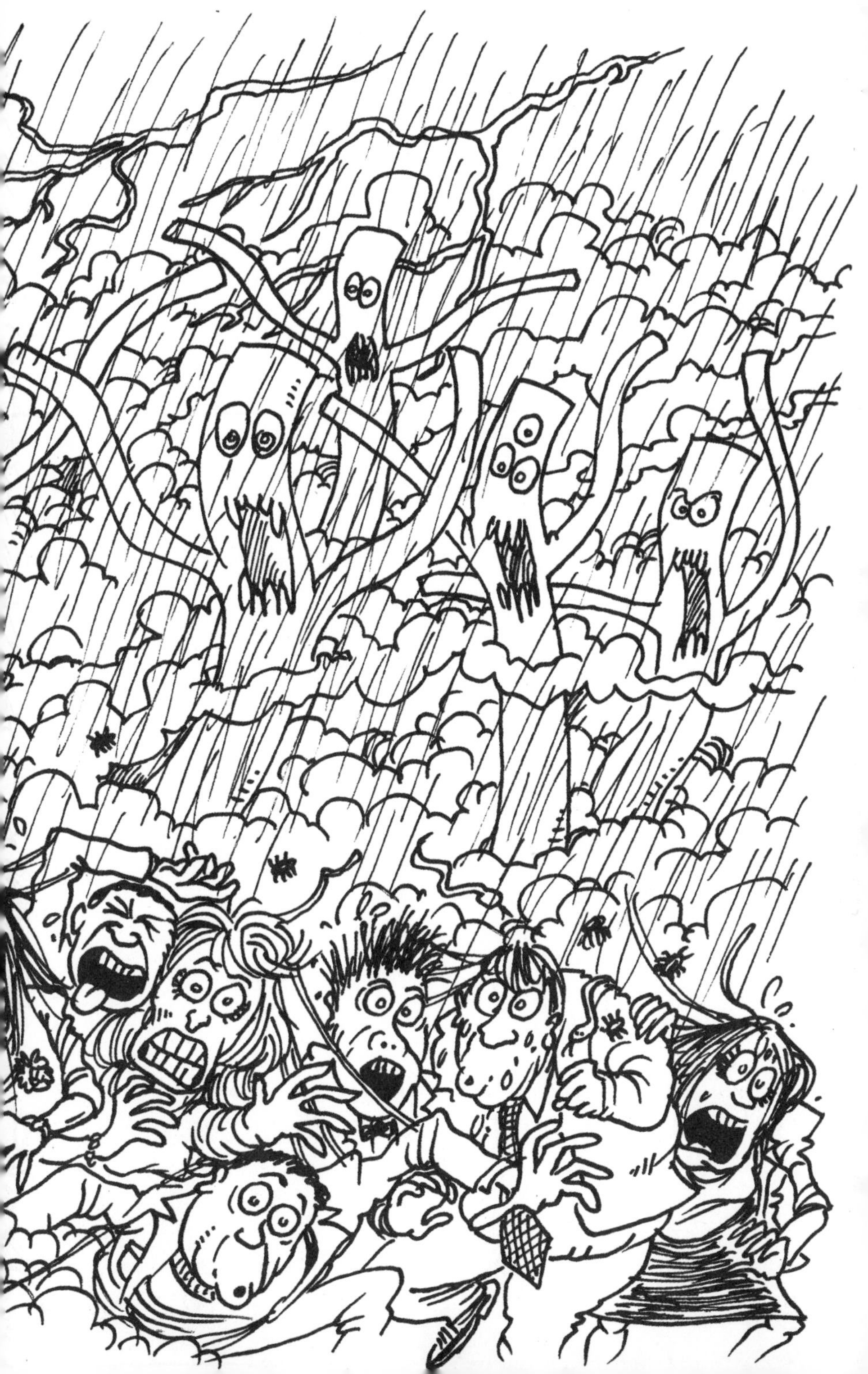

It's complete pandemonium! The audience is shouting and screaming and waving their arms as the fog and thunder and lightning and rain and heavy metal music and confetti and silly string and giant monsters fly all around them!

A totally epic monster magic success!
But there's still one more order of business.

"OK, Jasper and Jessup," I shout into the mic, trying to be heard over the noise and music, "lower me down."

This harness the Wickerstools borrowed from the Garvanni trapeze team (I told you they knew everybody!) is really cool. The twins can fly me anywhere over the chaotic audience. But I have one particular destination in mind . . .

"So I figured I'd go out with a bang!"

My sister, Rachel, and Leesa Needles both got their own paint-filled balloons, too . . . but that's not as great as I thought it would be.

Don't get me wrong. It's pretty cool dishing out my monstery payback to the ones who have it coming. But the really awesome thing . . .

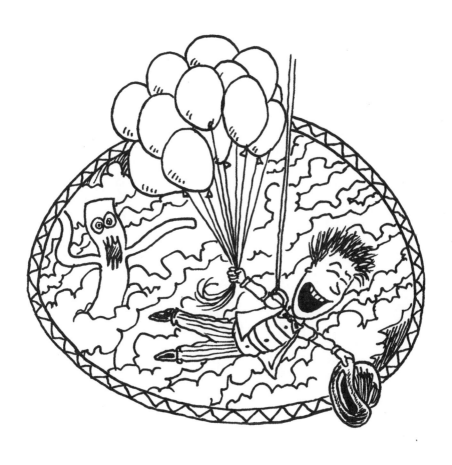

. . . is just being myself again!

30 THE END OF IT

As the screaming and the monster effects die down, I float toward the stage to face the music. But first . . .

I settle on the ground and grab the mic. Jasper takes my balloons, and Ricky gives me a spotlight.

As if I didn't already have their attention.

"And I'd like to give a very special shout-out to the one man without whom none of this would be possible . . ."

The crowd just stands there in stunned silence. And then suddenly they break into wild cheers and start clapping!

The enthusiastic crowd carries a dumbfounded Mr. Needles onto the stage and drops him right next to me.

Mrs. Badonkus, the school principal, comes bounding onto the stage clapping. She's soaked to the bone, covered in silly string, rubber snakes, plastic spiders and roaches . . . and grinning from ear to ear!

DESMOND PUCKET! YOU DID IT, MY BOY! YOU MADE OUR JUNIOR HIGH MUSICAL INTO SOMETHING PEOPLE WILL ACTUALLY WANT TO COME AND SEE!

She shakes my hand excitedly.

"I'm scheduling extra performances!" she continues. "When word about this gets out, we'll sell a million tickets! The school will make a fortune!"

Suddenly, pushing through the crowd onto the stage . . .

If you could hook Tina to a generator, that girl could light a small city.

A hug from Tina Schimsky! And she called me her "little balloon man"! Does this get any better?!

Mrs. Badonkus grabs Mr. Needles again.

"If this show takes in as much loot as I think, he can go on any field trip he wants!"

"One more thing, Needles," the principal adds. "I want you personally to chaperone Pucket on that trip."

"The way you and Desmond get along is an inspiration to the entire school! From now on I want you guys as close as two peas in a pod!"

Great.

Not exactly the happy ending I was expecting . . .

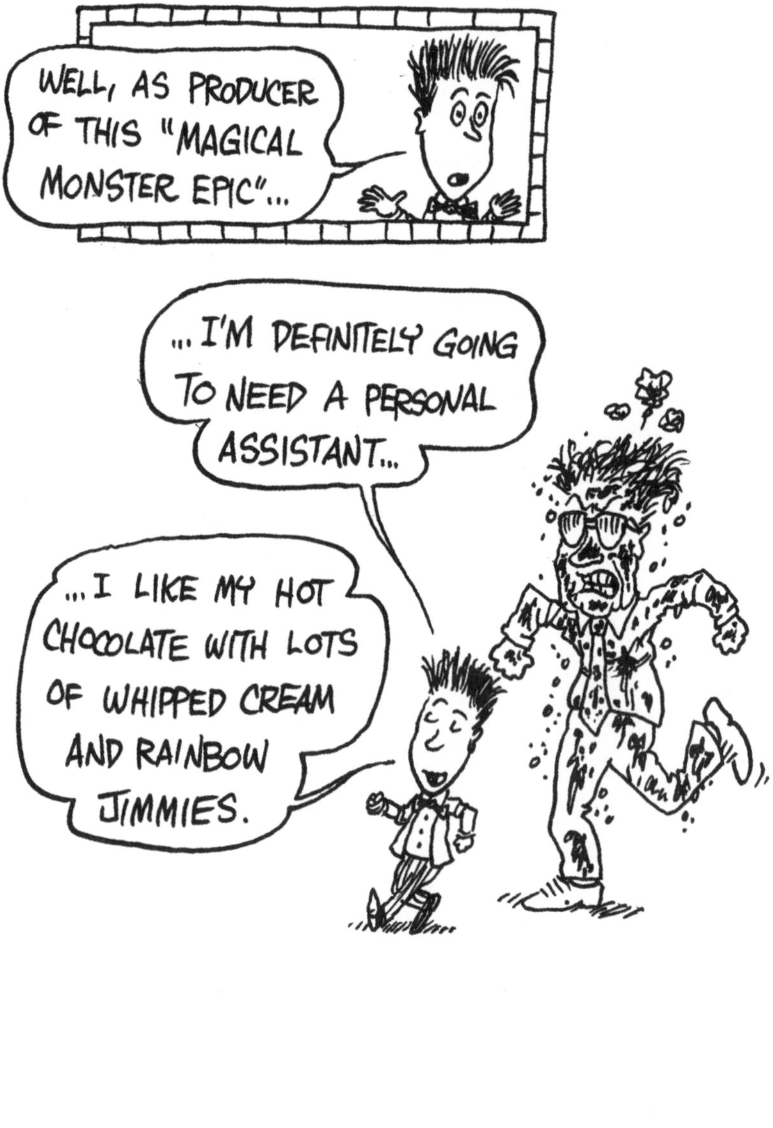
WELL, AS PRODUCER OF THIS "MAGICAL MONSTER EPIC"...
... I'M DEFINITELY GOING TO NEED A PERSONAL ASSISTANT...
... I LIKE MY HOT CHOCOLATE WITH LOTS OF WHIPPED CREAM AND RAINBOW JIMMIES.

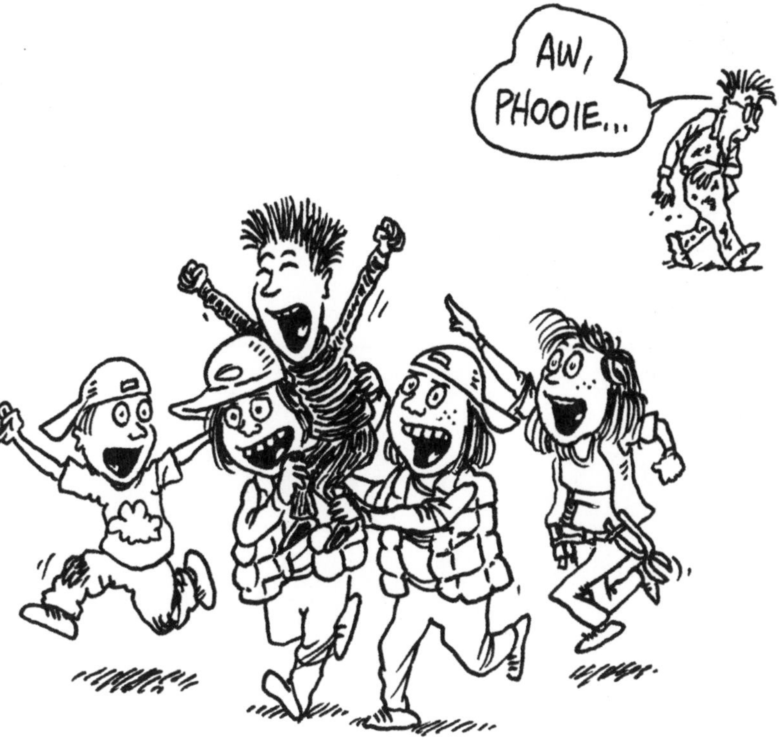
AW, PHOOIE...

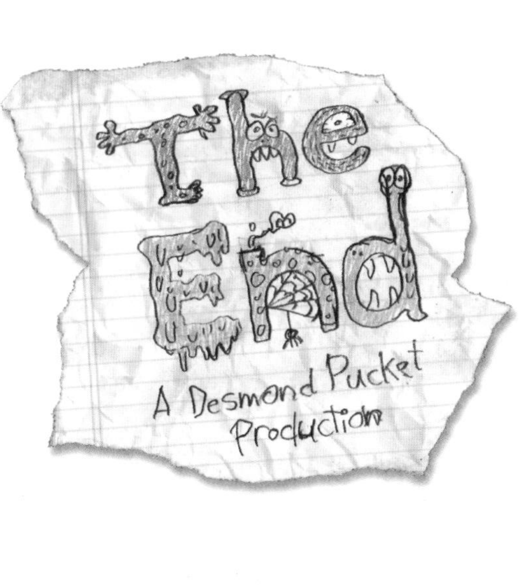
The End
A Desmond Pucket Production

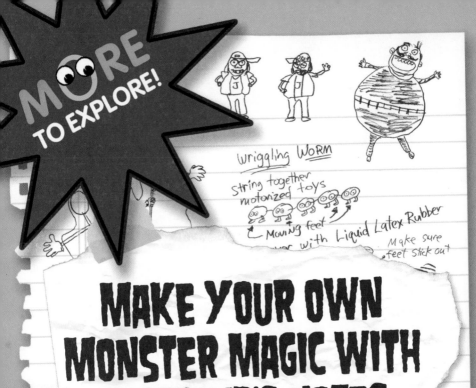

Wriggling WORM

String together
motorized toys

← Moving feet

with Liquid Latex Rubber

Make sure
feet stick out

MAKE YOUR OWN MONSTER MAGIC WITH DESMOND'S NOTES

The Toilet Goblin

Goblin attached to seat

When toilet is opened, Goblin comes Out!

DESMOND PUCKET

Desmond's Easy-to-Make Fake Blood Recipe

You Need:

 ← CORN SYRUP

 ← Red Food Coloring

 ← Chocolate SYRUP (OPTIONAL)

① In a plastic bowl, add a bunch of corn syrup, then a squirt or two of red food coloring and mix.

↑ corn syrup

← Red food Coloring

②

③ Add some drops of chocolate to make it deep, dark red

 ✳ BE CAREFUL WHERE YOU use this blood !! it can stain clothes and furniture!! ✳

 FUN FACT: The blood in the movie "PSYCHO" was really chocolate syrup! They made the movie in black-and-white, so it looked like real blood! Did you know that?

DESMOND'S NOTES

FUN with SOUND FX!

How to make a cool Monster growl effect:

what you need:

A coffee Can (empty) of something shaped the same

Something to record with:

Microphone

① Put the recording thing or microphone into the can → and start to record

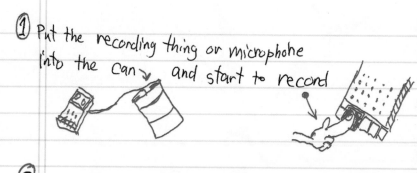

② put your mouth over the can hole and leave space for an opening to cover with your hand

③ Growl into the can as you move your face and hand to cover and uncover the can as your growl. Play back to scare. makes AWESOME growls!!

DESMOND'S NOTES

Desmond's Phantom Knocker!

This effect works best with a two-story house, you upstairs and your victim (heh, heh) directly underneath, downstairs.

What you need:

a long piece of string + a tennis ball or pinky ball

(1)

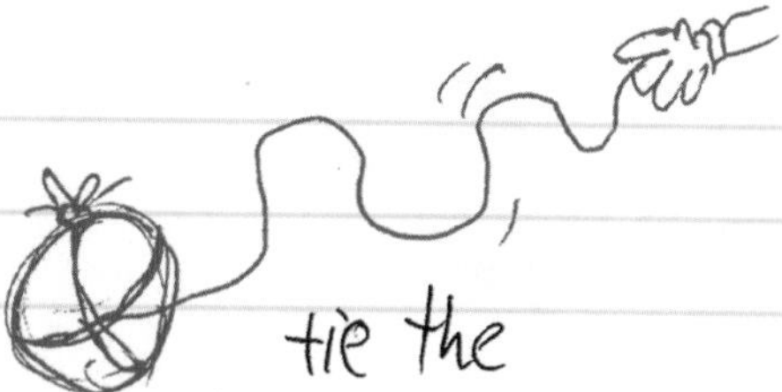

tie the String to the ball.

This effect also works great with "Desmond's Perfect Ghost"!

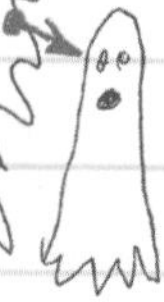

(2) throw the ball out of upstairs window holding onto the string

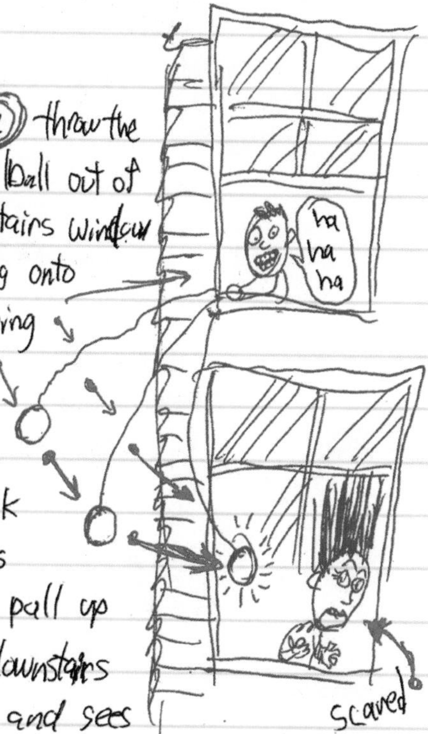
ha ha ha
scared

(3) let ball bank on downstairs window, then pull up fast! Person downstairs hears the noise and sees nobody there and gets scared! Repeat!

DESMOND'S NOTES

Desmond's Perfect Ghost!

What you need:

white curtain sheers - these are the light see-through curtains inside heavier curtains.

Styrofoam ball, about the size of a soccer ball

String

a broom stick

① The most important thing to make a perfect ghost is curtain sheers, because they are light and blow in the wind in a ghostly way. Maybe your mom has old ones you can have!

② Drape the sheer over the styrofoam ball.

you can even cut the bottom to make it ghostlier!

③ Attach the stick and string to the styrofoam ball, now make your perfect ghost fly!

WORKS GREAT with the Phantom Knocker!

DESMOND'S NOTES

A wretched Recipe

Desmond's Deadly Dolly Dessert

What you need:

Two boxes of gelatin dessert mix

a big bowl

can fit inside bowl

a weird doll (in this case, one of Rachel's favorites!)

① Prepare gelatin according to package directions (I picked cherry and lime because they make a sick color mixed together).

② half-way through the gelatin setting up, remove from refrigerator and push doll into bowl, face down. Put back in the fridge.

doll

bowl

③ After gelatin is fully solid, put bowl upside down on plate and let gelatin fall onto plate.

④ garnish with backyard leaves and serve to sister (or other dope!)

AAAAAA!

BE SURE TO CHECK OUT DESMOND'S CONTINUING ADVENTURES . . .

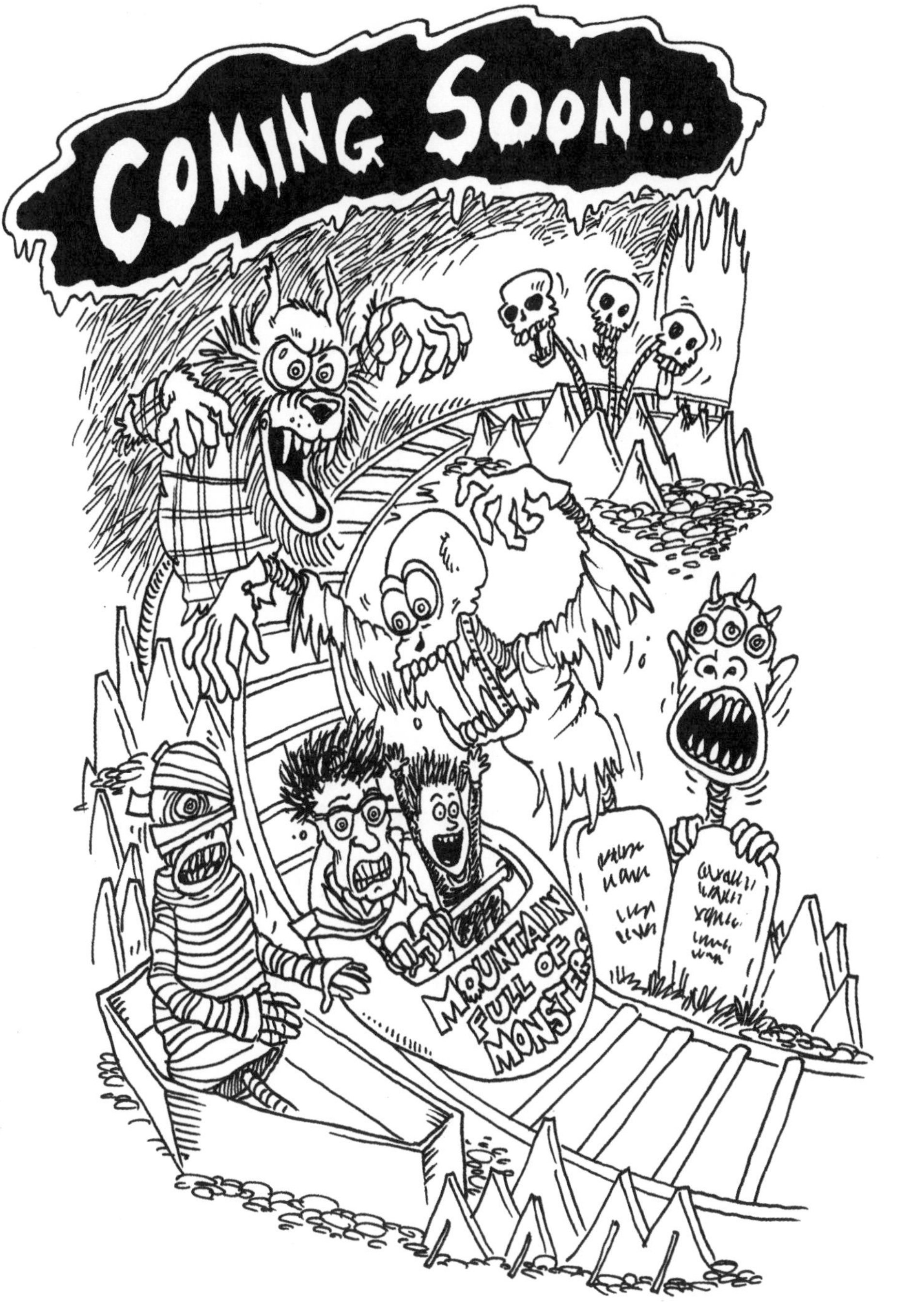

COMING SOON...
MOUNTAIN FULL OF MONSTERS

Andrews McMeel Publishing, LLC
an Andrews McMeel Universal company
1130 Walnut Street, Kansas City, Missouri 64106

www.andrewsmcmeel.com

13 14 15 16 17 SDB 10 9 8 7 6 5 4 3 2 1

ISBN: 978-1-4494-3548-6

Library of Congress Control Number: 2012956051

Made by:
Shenzhen Donnelley Printing Company Ltd.
Address and place of production:
No.47, Wuhe Nan Road, Bantian Ind. Zone,
Shenzhen China, 518129
1st Printing—7/15/13

ATTENTION: SCHOOLS AND BUSINESSES
Andrews McMeel books are available at quantity discounts with bulk purchase for educational, business, or sales promotional use. For information, please e-mail the Andrews McMeel Publishing Special Sales Department:
specialsales@amuniversal.com